The Girl with the Empty Suitcase

A NOVEL

KRYSTA MACDONALD

DEDICATION

For Brandon, who said I should, and knew I could.

And so now, I did.

CONTENTS

The Girl with
the Empty
Suitcase

CHAPTER 1

Danielle, age 12
1992

This is stupid. I mean, math is stupid. I totally get why I have to go to school and do homework and all that crap, but math? Come on. Last year it was okay, but Mr. Lane isn't my teacher anymore and now we are doing things that we will never ever ever in a million years use again. Mrs. Lutte is too nice, too. Funny, huh? A kid saying a teacher is too nice. Well, I mean it's not like it is a bad thing to be nice, but Ryan and Dawson made her cry again, and I think if she wasn't too nice they wouldn't do that. She does this stupid thing where she flicks the lights on and off to try and get us to shut up when we are being loud. It's kind of hard not to laugh at that. I mean, she must think we are six-years-old or something. So today in class Dawson called her a fat cow - she isn't, well, not fat I mean - and Ryan started mooing, and anyway, it is pretty hard to concentrate on figuring out what the hell "x" stands for when the teacher is crying and running out of the room and the boys are all mooing and the principal comes in and yells at us and we all get detention just because a couple boys can't figure out when enough is enough.

To be fair, when Ryan started calling her "Mrs. Butt" instead of Mrs. Lutte, I did laugh. It was funny. Kind of obvious, but funny.

I don't see when I will use math anyway. When will I ever have to "solve for 'x'"? They always say when grocery shopping. Funny, I have been grocery shopping with Mom since I was born and I have never seen any grown-up whip out a notepad and do an algebra problem while staring at a can of peas.

I wonder why Mom always does the grocery shopping and not Dad. Maybe it is a grown-up thing. Maybe when they got married they had a discussion about who would do what.

"Do you, Sharon, take this man to be your lawfully wedded husband?"

"I do, but only if he barbecues on Sundays and cleans up the yard and folds the laundry and pays the bills."

"And do you, Albert, take this woman to be your lawfully wedded wife?"

"Of course, provided she cleans the house and does most of the cooking and changes the diapers and buys the groceries."

I don't know, now that I am thinking about it, maybe that would not be that bad of an idea. Work out the expectations into the wedding vows, you know? Then at least everyone would know what they were getting into. I bet if more people did that, more people would stay married. Or at least not fight so much. Maybe Mom and Dad should have done that. Of course, then they would just find something else to scream about.

Or maybe not.

Jane's parents got divorced when she was six. I know divorce is supposed to be this God-awful, horrible thing, but I am not sure that is totally true. I sometimes wonder if Jane's parents have the right idea. She says she remembers them fighting, but only sort of. Now she and her sister spend every other weekend and most holidays with her dad. Her dad has this new girlfriend who lives with him and Jane says she is totally nice but she gets super touchy-feely with her dad which Jane says is gross and it totally is because it is her dad, but secretly I also think it is kind of nice. My mom sure isn't touchy-feely. Not that you want to see your dad being felt up or anything (oh my God, so gross!) but at least Jane knows someone likes her dad, which is, I don't know, kind of cool I guess.

Anyway, Jane has her thirteenth birthday next month. She says she is going to get two birthday parties! Isn't that awesome? Her mom is going to take us all out for dinner, and then we are going to a movie, and not a little-kid one either. Jane gets to pick, of course, which means she will pick something scary so she has an excuse to cuddle up to Jordan. Give me a break, right? Why can't girls just put their heads on guys' shoulders without having a scary movie on? Well those are the rules and nobody asked me about them when they were making those decisions, so whatever.

So she gets the dinner and movie. But then her dad and Trisha - that's his girlfriend's name I guess, and it is kind of weird to be calling a grown-up by her first name, but that is what we are supposed to do, so okay - they are going to have a whole spa thing at their place. I think Trisha is trying to get Jane to like her, and Jane thinks so too, but says she doesn't care that much. I guess Trisha is going to teach us how to do mud masks and her friend is going to come give us real manicures! I am super excited, and have already decided on blue polish.

When I told Mom, she kind of did that thing where she purses her lips together until they become a super thin line. And she raised her eyebrows and I got worried that she was going to say I have to stay home, but she didn't, she just muttered something about "homewrecker", which I guess she meant about Trisha, which is stupid because Trisha didn't move in with Jane's dad until two years ago or something, but there was no point me telling her that, so I just kept my mouth shut. I figured if I corrected her or talked back she would get mad again and then I might have to stay home after all.

This is so bogus. I don't get why teachers even give us homework. Especially math. Like, if I didn't get it at school, am I going to magically get it at home without Mrs. Butt there to help me? So instead of focusing on these numbers and whatever else, here I am, thinking about Jane and her parents and my parents and Ryan's hair. He has really nice hair. Of course he is way too cool for me, and also kind of dumb, but I would die - just die - if he knew I thought he had nice hair.

Oh right. Math. When I asked Dad about algebra he kind of chuckled and looked at my homework and shook his head and handed it back to me. Helpful, right? Then he started talking about how it is important that I "figure it out myself", and use my difficulties as "a learning opportunity". Which I know actually means he has no idea how to do any of this stupid math either, which I further know proves my point about how useless it is. If Dad can't remember how to do math and he is a grown up and works in a fancy office building, why do I have to know it when I am twelve? Well, twelve and eight months.

Jane is only a few months older than me but has started acting so smart. I mean, I know I do stupid things sometimes, but just because Jordan is her boyfriend and she gets two birthday parties, she thinks she is so worldly and mature. She actually said the words, "When you get to be my age..." Ridiculous, right?

Not that I am mad at her or jealous or anything, especially for the two birthdays thing, because after all, I benefit too. And I know splitting her time between two places is kind of brutal, but other times, I don't know. Just having one house like I do isn't that hot either.

Plus, parents are ridiculous. Like, Mom thinking I don't get the muttered "homewrecker" comment. Or when they think we can't hear them screaming at each other just because they shut - okay, slammed - the door. Voices carry, people. Or, like, a couple weeks ago when we were supposed to pretend everything was normal after Mom took off.

We were hanging out in the living room. I was sitting on the couch, drawing on my sketch pad. Grandma gave it to me and I have real artist pencils that go along with it. Anyway, I was trying to sketch the lamp in the corner - a "still life" - and Calvin was hanging out making a mess on the floor with his Star Wars toys. I know it was Star Wars because I remember the "pew pew" noises he was making when he was getting the characters to fight each other. That did not make sense, because he was simply bashing one toy against the other, slamming their heads together, not making them shoot each other, so why the hell was he making "pew pew" sounds?

Anyway, I was sitting on the couch, Calvin was on the floor, and when we heard the shouts starting from down the hall we just kind of looked at each other. Normally I try to get us out of there before the fight makes it as far as we are. I know Calvin can always still hear it, but if I can get us to the other corner of the house, maybe he can't always hear exactly what is being screamed. Like, the swears and stuff. Plus if they see us, one, or both, of them generally starts to bring us into it, arguing about us too. Like, about how the other one isn't a good mom or dad, and how dare they scream in front of the kids, which is just super funny if it wasn't so lame, because they are both screaming... Jane says that is what ironic means.

But this time we were not going to have time to leave the room, so when Calvin looked at me with his eyes all wide like he does, I just shrugged and nodded at his toys. If we can't escape, sometimes it works to blend into the furniture. Pretend we can't hear anything, can't see anything. Then they sometimes forget we are here.

Sure enough a door slammed and Dad called Mom a bitch and Mom called Dad a prick and there was more stomping and something being banged around and I scooted way to the end of the couch, far in the corner, like maybe they won't see me there. More stomping down the hall, this time again towards us. She came into view first, then him following her. She stormed right past the living room, right past us. Her eyes were all red and puffy, and his were, too. They had both been crying, which is weird because it was really quiet in the house before this last bit here, and usually she only cries when she is yelling and he is yelling back. Or that time when she was cleaning up the picture frame she threw that broke. But this time they had both been crying, then screaming, then storming around.

She didn't even look our way as she headed for the door. Another slamming sound, then Dad flinging it open, screaming her name out the door as her car peeled back out of the driveway and onto the street. I am sure people could hear that "Sharon!" all the way down the block. He stood there a bit, staring out, then slammed the door again. After that it was quiet, and Dad just leaned his forehead against that closed door. I could tell he was crying, and for some reason that made me even more uncomfortable than all the yelling and name-calling and throwing things, so I looked away.

After a while, I could hear him come into the room, but I did not want to look up. I knew he sat in his chair though, because I could hear him sort of fall into it. I could hear that he wasn't crying anymore, but he was still sniffling a little, and doing that thing where you try really hard to not be crying and sniffling so it just comes out super quiet but kind of choking, too, and he was taking deep breaths like he was trying to calm down. I don't know if he was looking at Calvin and me, as I wanted to seem very interested in my sketch. But after a bit I could hear Calvin shuffle a bit closer to Dad, so I thought it was safe to at least glance at him.

"Daddy?" Calvin's voice was a whisper.

There was no answer.

"Dad?"

Dad looked up at Calvin, but again did not say anything.

"Dad, is Mom coming back?"

I held my breath.

Dad sighed. "I don't know."

I was a little scared, I'll admit. Mom had never left before, and it was evening. I had made supper of course, because I always did, but that was before Dad had come home and this whole mess started, and now Mom was gone and I wasn't really sure when she would come back, and now Dad was saying he didn't know if she would come back at all.

I knew she would, though.

Last summer, we went camping. We have this trailer that used to be Grandma and Grandpa's. I like tents better because I think it is more like real camping, but Mom hates sleeping on the ground, so the trailer it is. At least we still get the campfire and we go the lake and there is this old rope swing that I dared Calvin to jump from last time and he started crying because he was too much of a baby. But anyway, back at the campsite, we were talking about Jane. Mom was saying that she didn't think she was a "good influence" on me, which is dumb because Jane is way prettier and smarter than me, and good at math too, so she is probably a really good influence on me, since she makes me want to be better than I am. I didn't want to argue with Mom, but at the same time, I didn't like what she was saying and knew I needed to defend my best friend.

"What is that supposed to mean?" I asked her.

"What is what supposed to mean, young lady? Would you like me to define the word 'influence' for you, or 'bad'? What exactly are you wondering?"

"Sharon, leave her alone," my dad muttered without really looking up from the fire he had been staring at for a while.

"Do not tell me what to do, Albert. She can answer for herself. What exactly do you want to know, Danielle?" Mom was staring at me now.

I breathed deep to control my temper, which I could feel rising. Some people say anger rises like the colour red moving from the tips of your toes up to the top of your head. It doesn't. When I get angry it is a tingling feeling, and it starts somewhere in my head, in the front of my brain, and I feel it move down through me, until I kind of feel numb, and empty except for that tingling feeling.

I did not want to lose my temper now, though, so I took a deep breath or two or ten, and evened my gaze, which I hope seemed calm enough, back at my mom, who certainly did not seem calm. "I am just wondering, Mom, why you think Jane is a bad influence on me?"

"You are a child, Danielle. You don't understand the world. She is from a broken home. That means she is trouble. Or at least she is going to be one day, probably soon. She doesn't have her parents at home watching her, so she's no doubt running wild."

"No she's not!" I blurted out. I instantly recognized my mistake.

"No?" Crap. There go those eyebrows. "No? Don't talk back to me, Danielle. You are twelve. You know nothing. Your little friend's father left her, just like he left her sister and her mother. If he can walk out on his wife and children, well, what kind of a man is that? And what kind of person can she possibly become in that life? It may not have been Jane's fault, but now she can run around and do whatever she pleases, and is spoiled and troubled because of it, and that is just the way things are, and the sooner you can wrap your pretty little head around that, the better off you will be."

Now, I know I do not know everything, but I also knew that this whole speech of my mom's wasn't right either. "Mom, Jane's dad left years ago. This isn't new."

"Exactly. And she has had all of that time to run wild."

"She doesn't run wild! She sees both of her parents. They both love her, they just don't love each other anymore. That doesn't mean she's wild."

"You don't know what you are talking about." Then, turning her attention to my dad, continued. "See what I mean, Albert? She wouldn't be such a brat and be talking back if she wasn't hanging around with that girl so much."

Dad sighed and finally looked at me. "Look, your mom actually has a point. Don't talk back to her. Jane seems like a really nice girl. But the fact is, when you promise to be with someone forever, you should mean it forever. I think Jane's dad didn't mean to be selfish, but by abandoning his family, he was. Divorce happens when people quit. And especially for Jane and Bethany, he should not have quit."

So I knew right then that my parents did not believe in divorce. So, when my mom stormed out of the house that evening, I knew she would come back. I was right, of course, since she was there the next morning, pretending like everything was fine, asking about my homework and if I would get Calvin's cereal ready. I was a little surprised to recognize that feeling of disappointment that she was there, standing by the coffee machine. I knew that every time Mom or even Dad walked out the door, they would come back.

But I wondered if they should.

CHAPTER 2

Danielle, age 17
1997

I am not really sure what to say about all of this. I mean, I feel like I should say something to Jane. We are supposed to be best friends, after all. But I do not want to tell her what happened. I mean, well, part of me does, but the other part really, really would rather not.

But she is sitting there, staring at me over a cup of coffee. Double-double of course. How very Canadian. Her hair looks way too good to have just come from the craziness that is outside. I swear it looks like she just came from the hairdresser - and not the main street place I go to for eight bucks a trim. I mean one of those fancy salon-type places, where you have to call for an appointment a month in advance and they bring you herbal tea while a team of stylists work magic on your split ends. She has this cute, bouncy, layered shaggy style - not just a haircut, but an actual style. It totally frames her face and is super cute. Meanwhile, I look more like a ten-year-old boy. I was going for a sassy pixie-cut. Instead I ended up with a short mess on top of my head that does nothing to hide my awkward features. I do not have Jane's adorable cheekbones, her sparkling eyes. How did she learn to do her makeup that way? I run my tongue over my own lips. It feels like I have a thick layer of wax on top of them. So much for cute gloss.

Jane's going on about something. Crap, I have to pretend I was listening. Let's see, let's see. Oh, her car. She must have driven it here, to this coffee shop that we have been to more times than I can count, first meeting for hot chocolates, then coffee that was really more sugar and cream than actual coffee. But that was then. Before.

"Can you imagine? Me sitting on the side of the road with a flat tire? Of course I told Vincent there was no way I was going to be some girl sitting around waiting for a boy to come pick her up or for some nice man to come save me. So I got him to teach me and now I know how to do it myself. Isn't that crazy?" Jane was looking at me, expecting me to say something.

"Vincent?" I offer lamely.

"Yeah, Vincent. I mean of course he was fine teaching me. You know, he is fine teaching me anything." She smirked. "But really, he is just so smart. I mean, of course he would have to be to actually be in college. And he said he would help me figure out the whole scholarship thing next year." She flips her hair back over her left shoulder and takes a sip of coffee. Afraid of staring, I focus instead on her coffee cup, cupped in her perfectly-manicured mint-coloured nails. Mint. My own nails are jagged, chipped, and surrounded by angry red skin, which I constantly catch myself picking and chewing. But Jane's are cool, collected, and mint.

"But Vincent said it was just a matter of doing something, you know? Something. Like, when you actually get to college all this" - she gestures around her absently - "this junk we deal with in high school, it all just goes away."

"Yeah, but Jane, that's not until next year. I mean, worrying about it now, doesn't that just, I don't know, make the rest of this school year seem worse?"

Jane is staring at me like I suddenly have developed a bad case of two-extra-heads-itis.

"I don't mean high school is my favourite thing ever or anything," I rush. Don't get me wrong. It's pretty awful. It's just, well, at least you have your shit pretty together. And it's not like life after high school is going to be easy. I mean, everyone loves you at school -"

"Not everyone," Jane interrupts, but smiles a smile that tells me that she knows just how true my statement is.

"I guess if I got the grades you do, I would be excited about college or whatever, too."

"Or whatever? You don't think you are going to college?"

"Oh I don't know," I shrug, hoping that I look like I don't care at all, like the idea of next year and the year after that and all the years after that doesn't terrify me, like I don't wish I had the power to stop or at least slow down the ticking hands of every clock in the world.

"Well of course you should go to college, Danny. Vincent says it is just the best time in the whole world. And there are so many smart people there, and you call all of your teachers by their first names, and it is just a creative outlet, which of course is so perfect for you."

"Me?" I try to make the question seem nonchalant, but it comes out as more of a squeak than anything.

"Sure. Like, with your art and photos and whatnot. Vincent says there are whole classes where you can study that stuff, and on-campus clubs and everything."

Oh he does, does he? Isn't Vincent just so smart? I want to roll my eyes at her. Of course Jane would be dating a college boy named Vincent. What kind of name is that, anyway? He probably plays the bongos and sips fancy cappuccino and writes poetry about his eleventh-grade girlfriend. Gag me.

But of course I don't say that. Of course I smile, shrug again, and say, "Oh I don't know. That sounds cool and everything. I guess I just don't want to decide everything right now. Live in the moment, you know?" *Please sound cool, please sound cool...*

"Oh, Danny, you are totally right! See, I told you you're smart!" Jane grins and is almost able to keep the patronizing edge off the lilt of her voice. "So anyway, on to something else. You said you wanted to meet for coffee. So what is it?"

"What is what?"

"Come on. The elusive Danielle calls me up and actually wants to meet me for coffee? Actually wants to grace me with her presence? Something must be up."

"What's that supposed to mean?"

"Oh, please." Jane pauses to bring her coffee cup to her lips. "You know you're not exactly a social butterfly."

"Oh?"

"Well, you're far from a loser or anything like that, either."

"Oh."

"For goodness' sake, don't be so sensitive. Vincent always says 'it is the quiet mind that has the most to say'. Doesn't that sound so smart? He's probably quoting some famous philosopher or something. I told you, you learn so much in college. So you probably just have a quiet mind."

"Oh."

"Oh, oh, oh." Jane's tone is mocking, but I know she is just being playful. I blush a little, but don't really mind I guess. "So spill it, Danielle. 'Sup?"

"It's nothing really." I pick at the corner of my thumb, then start to chew it. This is why I don't have cool mint nails. Jane's perfectly-shaped raised eyebrow cues me to stop.

"Well, that clears it all up then," she mocks. "Try again."

"It's just, well, I kind of, sort of started seeing someone."

There is a longer pause than I would have liked, then a sharp intake of breath. "Oh my god, really? That's awesome! Who is it? Someone I know? This is so crazy!"

"It's crazy?"

"No, I don't mean it like that. It's just - I don't know – it's super awesome!" Jane is gushing so much, I'm surprised every eye in the place isn't turned on us. "Okay, back up, you have to tell me everything."

No, I don't. Inwardly I rebel against the idea of sharing all these new secrets. Outwardly I offer a giggle. "Okay. What do you want to know?"

"Who the hell is he, for starters?"

"Well, he certainly isn't as cool as Vincent of course. He's just this guy I know. I was a counsellor with his sister out at camp last summer, and we met that way I guess. We just sort of kept in touch."

"And?"

"And nothing."

Jane's face falls. "Come on, Danielle. I'll admit, you are not the most socially or... well, romantically mature individual, but surely you have more to tell me than that. You aren't seeing someone if you've just kept in touch with him once in a while since summer." She flips her damn flouncy hair again. Maybe if she wore it in a less stylish way, it wouldn't always need flipping. "What are you, pen pals?"

I can feel the heat rising up my face. "No!" I'm surprised by my defensive reaction and take a breath to calm myself. "I mean, at first there wasn't that much to tell. We hung out a few times. I thought we were just friends. I mean, a lot of the time his sister or his friends or something was there, you know? We went to a couple movies, and we sometimes would end up sitting beside each other, but I didn't really think anything of it. And then I showed up to hang out with Annie - "

"Who?"

"His sister. Anyway, I showed up at her place a couple months ago, and she wasn't there. So it was just me and him."

"Hold up. All this happened a couple months ago and you're just telling me now?" I am surprised to see that Jane looks a little hurt at this thought. Then again, she is in the school musical. Maybe she is just a really good actress.

"It's not like I didn't want to tell you. I just didn't want to say anything until I knew there was actually something to say, you know? Didn't want to, like, jinx it or anything."

"Okay, if you say so." Jane's tone was more teasing this time. "So what happened? You went over…?"

"Right, well I showed up, like I said, and Annie wasn't there. And that was kind of weird but I just sort of figured she would show up or whatever, and he told me to come in and then we were hanging out, and then he just sort of kissed me."

"He kissed you?"

"Yeah."

"Where?"

"In the kitchen."

"No, loser. I mean, like, what? On the cheek? Lips? Neck? Did he give you a little kiss on your forehead?"

"Lips."

"Cool. Tongue?"

"I don't know."

"You don't know? Liar."

"It was a couple months ago."

"Sure, sure. And you have been having such regular make-out sessions that you lost track?"

"Well, not regular…"

Jane raises her eyebrows. "Slut."

I am pretty sure she is teasing, but I blush again anyway, and bite my lip, darting my eyes down at my empty coffee cup. I shift it from one hand to the other.

Jane is still talking. "So…?"

"So what?"

"Well, dish. Tell me about him."

"Well, he's nice. Quiet most of the time. Smart. Funny. I'm pretty sure he can quote every Monty Python movie."

"And that is a good thing?"

This coffee cup is sure interesting. I pick at the tiny chip on the bottom. "Sure. I mean, I like those movies." I shrug, and wish I had not mentioned something specific. General is better. "It's not a big deal. Anyway, he makes me laugh."

"He cute?"

"Sure. He has these super intense eyes." I can feel the

corners of my lips turn up a little. "Like, they're this deep brown colour. Super dark. And crazy dimples. And he smells really good."

"You smell him?"

"Well not, like, going up to him and sniffing him of course. That would be weird. Just, like, I notice that he smells good. His cologne or shower gel or something. I don't know."

"How's his bod?"

"Pretty good." Crap! Crap crap crap. Why did I say that? Did I give it away?

"You've seen his body?"

"We go swimming," I blurt out. "Well, I mean, we did. We have before. Gone swimming. Like, at the pool." I stop and take a deep breath before I make it worse. Well I sure played that cool. Not.

Jane smirks. "So you have gone swimming, have you? Okay." I release that breath I took and look at her as she continues. "Look, Danny, you don't have to tell me whatever you don't want to. But I am glad you found someone who makes you happy." *There you are, old friend of mine,* I think. Her voice drops a bit and she dips her head to peer at me. "And Lord knows you deserve to have a little fun."

I don't want to talk about whatever it is she is maybe trying to talk about, so I offer a little grin. "I am having fun, Jane. Thanks. And look, I'm sorry I took so long to tell you about him. It's just so unusual for me, you know? And I didn't want to bug you if it turns out there wasn't really anything to actually tell. Like, I didn't want to go and make a big deal about it, and then have it all end up being nothing."

"So what changed your mind?"

This is it; practically an invitation. If I am going to tell her, now is the time. Do I trust her? Do I trust myself to actually admit it to myself? I twist the necklace hanging from my neck - a cross, a birthday gift from my grandmother. I'm not super religious or anything, but the necklace is pretty, and I love my grandma, and just lately I've felt like I should be wearing it, I guess.

"You fidget a lot," Jane points out.

"I don't mean to." I stick my tongue out at her, but drop my hands to my lap.

A huge pause. She is still waiting for me to fess up, to explain why I decided that now is the time to tell her. Why now? I weigh the options. On one hand, I could tell her. I could open up. She could understand. We could talk about things and she could be supportive and make me feel better, less conflicted. She could be a shoulder, not that I am going to cry, but she could be that if I needed. She could giggle with me, and we could be close again, like when we were kids and I used to tell her my secrets over late-night phone calls, huddled under the blankets in my room.

"Jane," I could say, "I did it. We did it. And I don't know how to feel about it, and I want to talk about it. I kind of liked it but I feel like I shouldn't, and maybe something is wrong with me because I know it is bad. But I like him and he makes me smile and feel pretty. Well, as pretty as I can feel. But we talk and I think maybe I love him but I don't know how to know for sure and he says he cares about me but I don't really know if I believe him. And I just feel so badly that I don't really feel badly."

I could say it. All of it. It would be easy. She wouldn't judge me, would she? Open my mouth, let the words out. They are there, all of those words, bubbling up in my throat, asking to be confessed.

Here we go. Deep breath.

I look up. She is just sitting there, waiting for my answer. She never bites her lip, like I am doing now. Her eyes never waver from my face. She never picks at her own skin or chews those mint-coloured nails.

I smile at her. "It's just, I like him. I mean, I really like him. And I kind of wanted to dish about it, you know? Like, about how he is cute and stuff, and I just kind of thought it would be fun to talk to you about him."

"Do you love him?"

I shrug, looking around at the other booths before answering. "Honestly, I don't know. I have no illusions. It's not like i think we are going to live happily-ever-after or anything. Maybe it's too early to tell."

Jane nodded with all the sage wisdom of having a college boyfriend. "That makes sense." She tips her head again at me, studying me. "Danny, did you sleep with this guy?"

No escaping the question now. I raise my eyes up to meet her inquisitive stare. I don't shift. I look, straight at her, honest and open, and take a deep breath.

"No," I lie.

CHAPTER 3

Danielle, age 19
1999/2000

Today is New Years' Eve. Wait, is it only at night when it is officially New Years' Eve? Who decides those things? And why don't I know about them? Is there some sort of meeting, or maybe an assembly, like the ones we used to have in elementary school, where all the finite details of all the little things in life get decided? And why didn't I get an invitation to that meeting?

All these people are just losing it over the whole Y2K thing. I don't think there is much to it. The world will keep turning. We will wake up tomorrow and everything will be fine.

But what do I know? I see all these other people stocking up on canned goods and giant jugs of water and batteries of every shape and size, people who are smarter than me, more prepared, and then I wonder if maybe I should be doing the same. Should I be more worried than I am?

Christine doesn't think so, and she is pretty smart, so that makes me less worried about not being worried.

Well now I sound neurotic, even to myself. Awesome.

Christine is my roommate. I know most people roll their eyes at the whole idea of living with someone they have never met before, but I don't hate it. I guess I figured it was a guaranteed way to make at least one friend while I was at college. Or if not an actual friend, at least there would be one person who would be forced to interact with me every day in some way.

And now I sound pathetic. Even more awesome.

I remember when I first met Christine. She looked like a poster child for the college lifestyle: stylish, of course, but also totally understated and funky. I was so nervous to meet this girl, whose stuff had already claimed the far bed in our small campus room. I had wheeled my over-stuffed suitcase down the bustling hall, trying not to run into any of the teary-eyed mothers or stoic fathers or reluctant younger siblings. Friends were high-fiving and calling out nicknames, and amid all that cacophony, I was standing still, darting my eyes from the paper in my hand to the number at the door and back again. I checked. I rechecked. Did I knock? The room could be empty, and then I would be standing there, knocking on a door to an empty room. And how long should I wait and knock before I let myself in? Plus, it was my room. Should I really knock on the door to my own room? That could be embarrassing. I didn't know much, but I knew that I did not want the first impression that I made on the one guaranteed human interaction here at college, to be one of embarrassment.

On the other hand, she could be changing. Naked. Bidding a tearful goodbye to family members. Having a last liaison with an old boyfriend - or even girlfriend, I supposed. That would cause further embarrassment, and I tried to decide which was the worst outcome and best impression I could give, and the distance between those two.

I decided to go for casual, rapped on the door lightly – knock, knock – half a second before I turned the handle and let myself in.

No one there.

A moment of relief washed over me as I took in the room that would be my home for the next eight months: two identical beds, on opposite sides of the room, a window in between, with a pair of matching desks facing one another. She had a number of boxes and bags scattered on the far bed already, so I hefted my suitcase onto the other, trying not to feel annoyed that she hadn't waited to have a conversation with me about which bed I should take. Not that I cared or anything; it just would have been nice to have been asked.

I didn't snoop, but I did let my eyes drift over at her stuff. Several nondescript boxes were stacked on the floor, one on her bed. A shoulder bag, frayed, with buttons I could not read without venturing closer, rested against the box on her bed, and a patent leather jacket was haphazardly draped across it. I was immediately intimidated, and pulled at the sleeve of my powder-blue hoodie. I had tried on three outfits before settling on jeans and a hoodie, and I was regretting not dressing up more now, looking at that jacket. I had thought with driving three hours and lugging boxes in -

That reminded me. I still had several of my own boxes to bring in, and I had to hurry if I didn't want a parking fine that I couldn't pay. So I left my anxiety about meeting the girl who would eventually materialize into Christine, for the more purposeful anxiety about moving.

On the last of my three additional trips to the car, as I maneuvered through the busy hall and into our room, I finally saw Christine. She was bent, rummaging through one of her boxes, her choppy, dark brown hair falling forward, and she wore a black choker, red spaghetti-strap tank top, and blue jeans. She looked thin, confident, and popular. I was out of my league here.

"Hey!" she almost shouted as I paused at the door. She turned towards me and gave me a bright, open smile. "You must be Danielle! I looked your name up on the register; God I hope that doesn't make me sound pathetic. Unless of course you aren't Danielle and then never mind. Here, let me help you with that." She took the box from my hands and set it down on the desk on my side of the room. "I hope you don't mind that I picked this bed. I can totally switch with you if you want. I haven't unpacked anything yet so totally feel free if you would rather have this one."

I relaxed at her bright rambling and overuse of 'totally'. "No, it's fine. I'm good here."

"I'm glad. Not that it matters to me. I am just glad that you're not someone who would throw a fit about not being on one side of the room. Or that we got off on the wrong foot. How much would that suck?"

Was I supposed to answer? The question sounded rhetorical, so I left it alone, which was apparently fine, as I wouldn't have had much of a chance to answer anyway before Christine started talking again.

"So anyway, I'm Christine. Did you have family here? Oh God, I'm not keeping you from some emotional goodbye am I?"

I finally smiled. "No, it's cool. I just came on my own this morning."

"See now, that's awesome. Me too. I figured, if I'm going to do this whole independent student thing, I may as well start that way. Plus Mom was working and I didn't need to ask her to take time off work just to hold my hand or something."

"I get that," I agreed, hoping to sound like I really did come here because of my own independence, and not because of some deep-rooted parental issue.

"Well, we can talk about decorating our room and stuff if you want. I kind of like the old traditional, my half, your half, but it's up to you, too. I kind of hope we get to be friends. I know you're not supposed to say shit like that, but it's true, and I am not a big believer in playing games or being subtle. Life's too short and all that, you know?"

"I think that's really cool," I said, and meant it.

"Me too. Obviously," Christine said, and smiled again.

Christine ended up being pretty alright for a roommate.

Things were not perfect, but so far, despite a very tense week or two in October, we got along quite well, and our mutual hope for friendship seemed pretty assured. She's more outgoing while I'm more quiet, but she isn't frivolous or snobbish, not a party queen or a stick-in-the-mud. We went out, sometimes alone and sometimes together, and it was her idea that I put up some of my pictures in our room, and join the photography club during Frosh Week.

So, when Christmas rolled around and I had to decide between hanging out with Christine, who was staying because her band had a gig over the break, or heading back home to sit around while my mother cooked and my father worked and neither pretended that anything was wrong, it wasn't much of a choice. I was pretty sure that my parents had not spoken directly to one another in the year leading up to my moving out, and Calvin was always off with his friends now anyway, so I really had no desire to put on a happy face for that. I decided I would stay with Christine.

And that is how I ended up letting her talk me into going to a big party tonight. One of the bars we frequent – not quite a college bar, but close enough to campus it usually is used as one – is having a big blow-out for the event. "It's only the millennium once!" she had said, when I hesitated about the party. "Are you really going to tell your children, and your children's children, that you spent the biggest New Year's celebration of your life hanging out in pajamas in your dorm room?"

"I highly doubt my children and my children's children will care one iota how I spent one night when I was nineteen."

"Forget it. You're coming. No arguments."

When Christine said "no arguments", she meant it, and that is how I ended up staring at my open closet, trying to figure out what one wears to a huge party. It had to be the right combination of sexy and sophisticated, fancy yet durable enough to undoubtedly get beer spilled on it. It had to be perfect for an occasion where I may hook up with my dream man, or may be forced to wear for all eternity when civilization as we knew it ended and I had to resort to a life of looting and crime. These options, though, seemed equally unlikely, so I resorted to a safe black dress, with spaghetti straps and a v-neck. It was slinky and had a little shimmer, but was not revealing, and I actually felt okay in it, so I slipped it on, and put my hair in a messy bun, teasing the ends to stick out all over the place.

I was touching up my makeup when Christine came into the room from the bathroom down the hall wearing a black maxi skirt and pink crop top covered in sequins. I wish I had the body to pull off something like that. I repressed the urge to pinch my sides and belly in frustration, instead telling her that she looked great.

"Damn straight I do. We both do. Now come on, we're leaving," she said as I tossed an extra lip gloss in my little purse, and gave myself one last look in the mirror. *Come on*, I said to myself. *You will have fun. You will be sophisticated and not a crazy dork. You will be talkative and smart and entertaining and sexy. You will not stand shyly against a wall the whole night. This will be awesome!*

To be fair, I have not been standing shyly against a wall the whole night. I have been sitting on a couch. I did first wander a bit, laughing politely at a pretentious joke or two, engaging in some small talk about the band, the ambiance, the city. I held up my glass and sang "Auld Lang Syne" off key after the countdown, the punk rock group on stage attempting some horrible modern rendition while we all screamed the more traditional words and tempo. I laughed with everyone else when someone flicked all the lights off and on. And then the band started up again, and I found the corner of a couch and perched on the armrest. Sitting would be more comfortable, but that comfort seems somehow defeatist. And here I can sit straighter, hopefully lessening the overall image of my chubbiness.

Periodically I get up, grab another drink, scan the room for

Christine, and then return to my perch. There I drink said drink, and look around, pretending to be aloof and not awkward. And then I invariably find that I have finished my drink, and for something to do I get another one, and that is how I end up drinking quite a bit.

Eventually I become aware that someone is trying to get my attention. I look over at the speaker and find a man sitting in a chair near me. He is a man - not a boy. He has to be mid-twenties, maybe even thirty, wearing dark blue jeans and a white button-up shirt left open to reveal a tight black t-shirt. He has stubble - actual stubble - and blue eyes that are startling paired with his dark hair. Or maybe that effect is just due to my high alcohol intake.

"Some band, huh?" I say smoothly. He smiles, and I figure I must have won him over with my wit. This is it. This understated yet undeniably sexy man is going to be so smitten with me that he will confess his attraction, then his love, and we will be married within a year, and everyone will say I am too young and it is too fast, but when you know, you know, and he will always say that he knew the moment I drunkenly asked him about the band at a New Year's party.

"Yeah," he says. "That's why I commented on them a few minutes ago." Poof! There goes that hallucination.

"You did?"

"I did."

"Oh wow. I'm sorry. Did I say anything back to you?"

"No, not really."

"I'm quite the conversationalist, aren't I?" Except I am not entirely sure I pronounce "conversationalist" correctly the first or even fourth time I attempt it.

He chuckles. "You having fun?"

"Oh sure." I stab at the ice cubes in my drink. "You?"

"Yeah, just here to pick up my little brother. I don't generally make a habit of hanging around eighteen-year-olds."

"Hey! I'm not eighteen!"

"No? How old are you then?

"Nineteen."

"My mistake." His smile is warm, and good-natured, and only a little teasing.

My brain realizes I sound like an idiot, but it has yet to communicate that to my mouth. "So if you are too cool to hang out with us kids, why are you sticking around here?"

He looks around, then leans in a little. "Honestly? I love the band." He winks. Holy hell. Is this guy - this man - flirting with me? No way. Impossible.

I shake my head. "You're teasing me."

"I am?"

"Save it, okay?" Warmth creeps up my neck. I'm getting defensive, I know, but I can't help it.

His smile falls. "I'm sorry. I didn't mean to offend. I just thought -"

"I know what you thought. You thought a drunk kid is sitting here all pathetic and you would come babysit. Well thank you but no thank you. I can take care of myself." And with that seemingly assertive declaration, I glide to the bar and order another drink, hoping that Christine will soon be ready to go home, but knowing that I will be forced to wait around another hour or two at least.

CHAPTER 4

Mark 27
1999/2000

I want to kill Brett for making me wait around for him. I hadn't even planned on leaving Joe's, but when Brett called, I could barely hear him through the screaming and shouting and music in the background, and I figured it was better to come and get him and make sure he was safe than, well, not. He was calling me for a ride. New Year's Eve is always nuts, and with this one being the big one - well, what everyone says is the big one - I didn't think he needed to be taking any chances drunkenly wandering around or something. I knew where he was, or at least where he had been planning on being as of a conversation over coffee two days ago, and so when I could not hear a word he said, I hung up the phone, raised a toast to Joe and Janine, made my excuses, and slid behind the wheel of my truck. I had just traded in my old car for this beauty, and ran my hands over the steering wheel. "Thanks for not giving me any trouble starting tonight," I muttered under my breath to the truck. This was a far cry better than the prayer I used to have to repeat every time I turned the key in my old car, even in the warm spring, let along the frigid December - almost January - temperatures.

Loud music shocked my senses, courtesy of a new heavy metal CD. I usually remember to turn down or even off the stereo, but I suppose I had been too wired from the excitement of the evening to bother. No matter - I appreciated the bass pumping through me as I backed out of the driveway.

Joe and Janine just bought their first place, were just moved in, and hosting the big party tonight. More friends settling down. What a weird phrase, "settling down". I don't much like the idea of "settling", but I have no problem with what the phrase entails: The whole wedding/ house/ kids/ career-that-actually-pays-the-bills thing. More and more of my friends are doing it. Not all, but more every day, it seems; just enough that I'm noticing I'm actually a grownup.

And now this: driving to pick up my baby brother from some bar down by the college. It wasn't that long ago that I was the one getting crazy in a place like this, and I would be lying to say that there isn't a weird sense of nostalgia associated with the whole thing.

I found the bar, parked down the street, and made my way to the door. The guy playing bouncer at the front let me in when I explained what I was there for, though he looked at me closely, no doubt questioning my motives. I know of guys my age who hang around the college girls. It's not my thing, but to each his own. I have too much to do to play that game anymore. I guess the bouncer decided I was harmless, and after all, it was after one and the crowd had surely started thinning a little after midnight, so he nodded, and even held the door open for me. Long gone are the days of trying to talk my way into bars. Now, "Hey Kid, I need to see your ID," has been replaced with, "Anything I can help you with, Sir?"

I made my way through the crowd, peering at the teenagers crowded in groups and rubbing up against one another on the dance floor. After a while, I began to doubt that Brett was even there, and of course that's when I spotted him, leaning up against a cute blonde a little near the stage. I stood as close as I could while not being creepy, and waved him over when he glanced my way.

"What are you doing here?" While he shifted in time to the music, I could see the surprise on his face.

"You called me. I thought you might need a ride."

"I'm kind of in the middle of something here," Brett said, gesturing to the girl behind him, who stood where he left her, watching us. "Think you could come back later, Bro?" Bro? Wow, he really was drunk. Yet despite the high volume at which he had to shout, pointed annoyance dripped from his slurred words.

"Tell you what," I shouted back. "I'm gonna hang around here for a bit. See what's up. The band's not bad. Then when you're ready to go, I can drive you."

"You don't need to wait around."

"How about I give it an hour or so? If it sucks I'll ditch you and you can find your own way back to Mom's."

"Suit yourself," Brett shrugged and turned back to the blonde.

Great. Now I have to find something to do that isn't leering after my brother and his barely-legal date for the night. I make my way to the bar, order a rye, and scan the room for an unobtrusive spot where I can see the dance floor, but not in a chaperone-type way. Over along one wall is a set of couches and chairs that are uninhabited, save a couple very much lost in one another on a love seat - how cliché - and a quiet conversation going on between a small group that have moved a few of the chairs into a circle near one of the couches. I settle myself on another chair, sort of near a girl in a black dress who I thought was part of the group. I didn't mean to eavesdrop, but have to fight a scoff when I hear their topic of conversation - the philosophy of politics. They are clearly trying way too hard to be intellectual college kids.

I listen to the music and sip my drink. Had I really been a part of this once? It seems impossible, yet I know it's true. I know I too had once leaned in to whisper to cute girls on the dance floor, discussed philosophy and politics (though I'm not sure if I ever analyzed them together), and swore that a great band was the best thing on Earth. I, too, had stressed over deadlines, and student loans (okay, I still kind of stress about those) and my next date. But now things have shifted. I have to fight to see myself in these faces. Instead I see my own students, who have already started filling out college application forms and asking for letters of recommendation. I'm not sure when this crazy shift happened, but it has, and I can't say I'm entirely sorry to be separated from all this chaos.

Looking around, I catch the eye of the girl in the black dress. I had thought she was part of the political philosophers, but I realize that she in fact is facing slightly away from them, seeming to concentrate instead on the ice cubes in her drink. I don't want to seem like I'm staring at her, so I make some comment about the band, to which she nods, shouting something that sounds like "good", gets up, and walks away.

She returns before the end of the song, carrying a full drink of something red and fizzy, of which she is making pretty short work. If I drank that fast I'd have a hell of a headache tomorrow, but she's young, so maybe it won't affect her.

Suddenly she turns to me and smiles. "Some band, huh?" She trips over her words.

I furrow my eyebrows, confused. Is she mocking me, or just really, really drunk? "Yes," I say carefully, leaning in a bit to reduce the shouting. "They're pretty good. That's why I commented on them a few minutes ago."

Now it's her turn for confusion to traipse across her face. Okay, not mocking; just drunk. "You did?"

"I did."

"Oh. Did I say something impressive back to you?"

"Not exactly," I smile.

"I'm quite the conversationalist, aren't I?" Her tone is self-deprecating, walking the line between teasing and outright flirting. She grins back at me then - a real grin, unassuming, just on the verge of laughing. Wow. She's beautiful, I can't help but think, and am immediately surprised by that reaction. I shake my head, so I can clear my mind without her thinking I'm disagreeing with her.

"Are you having fun?" I ask.

She turns her attention to the ice cubes in her nearly-empty drink. This is flirtatious alright. Reel the guy in a bit, laugh with him, then turn coy. Well, damn it, it's working. She has my attention.

"Yeah, just kind of here to pick up my little brother. I don't generally make a habit of hanging around eighteen-year-olds."

"Hey! I'm not eighteen!"

"No? How old are you then?" I lean a little closer. *What am I doing? What the hell am I doing?*

"Nineteen."

"My mistake." I can't help it. I smile again.

Her eyes search my face, then narrow. "So if you are too cool to be here with us kids, why are you hanging around?"

My head tilts, and I lean in so close we won't have to shout anymore. It is harmless, but there is a fierceness and sass behind those glaring eyes that is damn sexy, and I'm not ready to lose the chance for conversation with the one person here - besides maybe the bartender and the bouncer out front - who isn't looking at me like I am a creepy old man. "Honestly? I love the band."

She shakes her head so intensely that a few pieces of her hair fall down. "You're teasing me."

I realize by her tone that I have misspoken, overstepped, read all the wrong cues and responded in all the wrong ways. "I'm sorry. I didn't mean to offend. I just thought -"

"I know what you thought. You thought a drunk kid is sitting here all pathetic and you would come babysit. Well thank you, but no thank you. I can take care of myself." And with that, the mysterious girl in black gets up, teeters a bit, and takes off to the bar to get another drink.

I blink. Well, aren't I a piece of work? I just totally offended some girl, for no reason. So much for me not being a creep.

I let my eyes follow her at the bar, as she orders, smiles, and sips, and I reprimand myself for being such an idiot. I watch as she sets her drink down, turning to talk to a cute brunette in a crop top who steps up behind her. They clearly know one another, are good friends even, and the brunette is with some other people. *Well, that's enough of that*, I think, and am about to turn my attention back to Brett, when I feel my gaze freeze and harden into a stare. There is a young guy - of course everyone here is young - shifting himself closer and closer to where the girl in black is standing, her attention on her midriff-showing friend. It seemed subtle enough at first, but the way he keeps looking at her, and then looking at the bartender, seems off to me. I recognize him as one of the political philosophy debaters.

Black-dress-girl turns back to the bar and takes a drink from her glass. The boy takes half a step away. She turns to her friend again. The boy steps closer.

Something isn't right.

I stand up slowly, my eyes never leaving the young man. He shifts again, and now he is so close, I'd be surprised if he wasn't touching her. No crime in that of course, especially in this crowd, where it's impossible not to be touching the people around you. Still, I take a tentative step away from my chair and toward the bar. And that's when he reaches in his pocket, takes something small out, and drops it into her drink.

I reach him in an instant. "Hey!" I shout.

The girl's eyes flare as she turns around and sees me. I don't care though. I grab the prick by his shirt and pull him easily towards me. "You want to explain what you're doing there, bud?"

"Hey, man, let go. I ain't doing nothing."

In my mind plays the old joke I tell my students about double negatives, about all the English teachers sitting on a jury when the perpetrator insists that he "didn't do nothing", and all of the teachers nod to hear the confession.

"Try again." I'm snarling, yet praying that this pathetic excuse for a human doesn't have a group of frat-boy types gathering behind me, ready to jump in and save their buddy. I haven't been in a fight since the seventh grade, and I have no desire to start now.

"Look, I didn't mean nothing by it." He is stammering, looking around at the attention we are starting to gather.

"What's going on?" The bouncer from outside is beside us now, and he is not impressed.

"Buddy here thought the young lady's drink needed a little something extra when she wasn't looking. A little something like a pill he was dropping into it when I caught him."

I can hear the gasp from the girl, but I don't take my attention away from the face of the boy in my grasp, who's becoming more pale by the minute.

"You kidding me?" Mr. Bouncer is booming. Even in the dark I can see the red of his anger spreading across his bald head. He grabs the boy from me. "I'll take it from here."

"I...I...I d-didn't -"

"Shut up." The bouncer is seething as he half-pulls, half-drags the stuttering boy to the door.

"What's going to happen to him?" I call as I hurry behind.

"That's for the cops to figure out. Jim's callin' 'em now." He nods toward the man behind the bar, who's already on the phone, gesturing, his forehead furrowed. "Them's the procedures. In the meantime he's gonna wait out for 'em with me and Mike." He doesn't explain who Mike is, and I don't ask. "Now Mike's got a little girl, see, five or six now. Since she came along he's been super protective of the girls here. And Mike's also got one hell of a temper. Buddy here better hope Mike don't figure out what you caught him at, or he is going to have a very uncomfortable wait for them cops." He yanks the boy up the steps toward the door. "Stick around, 'kay? Case the cops wanna talk to ya or whatever."

"Sure." I don't know what else to say. I don't exactly feel that roughing the guy up before the police show up is a good idea, but at the same time I don't feel sorry for the guy or anything, either. And I have to admit that I envy Mr. Bouncer and this Mike fellow for getting to express their anger in a way I know I can't. "Well," I at last say, "Thanks."

"Nah, man. Thank you. Go talk to Jim. Go get a drink from Jim. On the house. And if he don't offer it to you, it's on me."

I thank him again and turn back to the bar, but I don't want a drink at the moment. I am actually more shaken up than I care to admit. Before I get to the bar, though, Brett comes running up, blonde in tow.

"What the hell happened, man? People are saying you saved some girl from getting roofied. That true?"

"Don't know. I guess so."

"Holy hell. Everybody!" Brett is shouting, but it doesn't seem like it's directed to anyone in particular. "This guy here - this guy - he's a damned hero. That's my brother, man. A hero!"

"Okay, Brett. Shhh. It's fine. It's not a big deal."

"Um, yes," a voice joins in from beside me, a voice decidedly more timid than the last time it was directed at me. "It really was a big deal." Her hand is resting against her throat, her eyes wide. "I don't know what to say. How can I thank....? If you hadn't seen him…"

She trails off, and her brunette friend is beside her, arm around her, as the girl in the black dress, who I had horribly offended and then evidently saved, all within the course of ten minutes or so, stares at me. I see the wetness waiting to spill over, but she doesn't blink away the tears that threaten, just levels those eyes at me. They are hazel, they are staring, and I am transfixed.

Maybe it's a hero's complex that keeps me talking to her. That's a thing, isn't it? Hero's complex? Anyway, she wants to buy me a drink to say thank you, but I refuse, insisting that I get her one instead, maybe to calm her nerves.

"No thank you," she shakes her head. "I think I've had

quite enough for one night."

Her friend keeps repeating, "Let's get you home," in a just-audible whisper, as she sizes me up, calculating, unsure, yet also appreciative.

"Look," I say as the black dress is allowing herself to be ushered out the door, her friend saying her goodbyes to those gathered around her, "I know this is probably totally inappropriate. But if you ever want to talk about what happened, or anything, or whatever, feel free to call me, okay?" I open my wallet and take a slip of paper out - a receipt for something or other - and write my number on it, then hand it to her. "If you never want to see me or talk to me again, don't feel obligated or anything. Feel free to throw that number away."

"I won't do that."

"You won't call, or you won't throw my number away?"

"That last one."

Her friend is back, holding a coat, putting it around the girl's shoulders. She keeps looking at me.

"I'm Mark, by the way."

"Danielle."

And then they leave, and if either of these girls would have looked back, they would have seen me staring after them, completely confused about what had just happened.

CHAPTER 5

Danielle, age 19
2000

It still feels unreal. If Mark hadn't shown up that night... I shudder every time I think about it.

Everyone hears the stories. The girls who set their drinks down, the ones who wake up in a strange beds, the ones who disappear, the ones who are never found.

I could have been one of those ones.

I think I was in shock after that. Christine was super nice of course, but after a day or two of sitting in my sweatpants eating junk food, I decided I was just feeling sorry for myself. Nothing had happened, after all. Sure, something *almost* happened, but it hadn't. Christine told me to take more time for myself, talk to someone, don't rush, but it just didn't feel right to me. I didn't want to make a fuss, I guess, which Christine said was stupid, but there it was. Besides, cleaning our room, reorganizing my clothes, and getting ready for the new semester actually made me feel better. And I started using different techniques in the dark room, and the focus on that helped, but still, every time I thought about that night, it was like an icy breath on my neck, sending shivers right through my core.

A couple weeks after, I was sitting at my desk, lining up some random items for a series of photographs. Classes had started, and I was throwing myself into projects and assignments.

"You don't go outside to take your pictures anymore?" Christine asked.

"I do sometimes."

"I haven't seen you outside except to cross the campus for class. I hardly even see you outside of this room."

"I've been busy."

"There isn't another reason?"

"Not that I know of."

"Then come out with us tonight."

I could feel the blood drain from my face and pool somewhere in my racing heart. "No thank you."

"Come on, Danny. You can't hide in our room forever."

"I'm not hiding. I just don't want to go out tonight. And I'm busy."

"You're sure?"

"Sure."

Christine sat on the edge of my bed, watching me move a pencil left, right, then left again. She didn't say anything, but I could tell she wanted to.

"You may as well say it."

"What?"

"Whatever it is you want to say. I can tell you're biting your tongue."

I could hear an intake of breath, clearing of throat. "Look at me, Danny."

I paused in my fidgeting, then glanced at her.

"Have you even told your parents what happened?"

My gaze shifted to my hands. "Nothing happened."

"You know what I mean. Now, I know you and your parents aren't super close or anything, but I'm worried about you. You're different is all. Different than you were before."

"Wouldn't you be?" I snapped my head back up to stare at her, even and unwavering and so uncharacteristic of me. "In case you haven't figured it out yet, I don't particularly like talking to my mother, and I certainly don't need you acting like some surrogate one in her place."

"Okay, okay." Christine held up her hands. "I'm sorry. I did say you needed more time. So I don't mean to rush you or pry. You know I'm here." She got up from my bed, seemed about to say something else, hesitated, then added, "You sure you won't come out with us tonight?"

"Not a chance."

"Okay. Just try not to stay at your desk all night. Grab a coffee or something."

I didn't look at her as she grabbed her coat, but I heard her keys drop into her purse, then the door open and close. Unaware I had been holding my breath, I let it all out in one long *whoosh*. I hadn't meant to snap at her, but snap at her I had. Stupid me. I never know how to act.

Grab a coffee, she said. Would it make me feel better for being so mean to someone who was only trying to be kind? I opened the door and peered into the hallway. Deserted. I closed the door again, breathing hard. I lifted the window. Dark.

This was ridiculous. I was nineteen years old and afraid to leave my own room. I *knew* that I'd be fine running to the coffee shop on campus. I *knew* that the chances of something happening to me during that time were practically zilch. My head knew that, anyway. My nerves, tightened throughout my body, were not so sure. I felt as though one of those nerves could so easily snap, splitting me up into so many little pieces.

I couldn't live like this.

Don't get me wrong; I wasn't desperate, not truly. I knew that awful things happened in the world, and what had happened to me - hadn't even *happened* to me - was infinitesimal in comparison. I also knew I couldn't cower in my room forever, ducking out only to rush to those classes I couldn't afford to skip.

I paced around. It didn't take me long to realize just how small this room was. I'm not sure I had noticed it before. I knew what to do.

His number was at the bottom of my purse, crunched up among the crumbs. I almost threw it out, thinking it was an old receipt of mine. But there was his name - Mark - and the seven-digits below it.

He answered on the third ring.

"Hello?"

"Hey, is this Mark?"

"Yeah."

"Hi Mark. It's Danielle." A pause. "I'm sorry, you probably don't remember me. We sort of met at a bar on New Year's. I was the one who... um... with the guy and... and you..." *Well this was going well.*

"I remember you."

"Great. I mean good." *Silence.* "What're you up to right now?"

"Working on some stuff."

"Oh, okay. I'm sorry, I didn't mean to bug you. I just found your number and thought... but it's okay..."

"Danielle, just a minute." He paused, and I waited. It didn't take long for me to convince myself he had hung up.

"Look, just forget -"

"Just a minute," he cut me off. Another pause, this one briefer. I could hear low conversation, and papers wrinkling. "Okay. Where are you? What would you like to do?"

I blinked. "Uh... Do you want to grab a coffee or something? I'm sitting in my dorm room."

"Sure. Do you want to meet somewhere specific?"

"Well, see, the thing is, it's just..."

"Do you want me to come pick you up?"

The relief was immediate and effective. "Yes, please. If you don't mind. I don't want to be trouble."

"No problem. I'll be in front of your building in, say, fifteen."

"Okay." Another pause.

"Danielle, you're going to have to tell me which building is yours."

"Oh, right." *Smooth, Danielle.* I told him, and hung up. The conversation had been a little weird, but I figured that was more my fault as his. But he was going to pick me up, and I was going to leave the room and prove to Christine - and myself - that I could still function as a relatively normal member of society.

Now, fifteen minutes later, I am waiting, as instructed, at the door to the building. It took everything I had to make the hurried walk from my room there, my eyes darting around, jumping a little at every sound. But I made it, and soon enough a truck pulls up, and the driver gets out and comes toward the building, and I recognize him in an instant.

"Hi." I say, and am only too aware of my jeans, my hair, my complete lack of make-up.

"Hey." He nods, and tilts his head in the direction of his truck. I don't say anything else, just follow him. He opens the passenger door for me, and I hoist myself up, fixing my gaze out the window, wondering what the hell I'm doing.

The way to the coffee shop is uneventful, and quiet, as is ordering - coffee for me, strong tea for him. "I can't sleep if I have coffee this late," he breaks the silence to explain. "Didn't used to affect me at all. Ah well."

We do the small talk thing for a while. I find out he's a teacher, and it strikes me that he's an actual, real grownup, with an actual, real, grownup job. "What made you decide to be a teacher?" I ask.

"Oh, the same as most people, I think."

"Summers off?"

He laughs. He has a great laugh, full and deep and loud. "Well, yes, that and the whole thing about it being super-rewarding, and inspiring kids, and all that."

"Do you inspire kids?"

He looks at me, and I know he's going to give me an honest answer. "You know what? I don't know, really. I try to, and I like to think maybe I succeed a little, but I don't think I have made any profound impact or anything. I haven't changed anyone's life."

"I wouldn't say that." Heat creeps over my cheeks as I heard the words coming from my own mouth. I shift my eyes down as I take a sip of the coffee. It isn't great.

He nods. "How are you doing, if you don't mind me asking?"

"Oh, I don't know. Fine I guess."

He tilts his head, waiting.

"It's just... I don't know. I get scared easy. And it's dumb, I know it's dumb, but I, like, freak out when I leave my room. Especially at night."

"You did sound relieved when I said I would come get you."

"Yeah."

"It's probably normal to be more scared than you were before."

"Is it?" I bite my lip. "Sure doesn't feel normal."

"Why's that?"

"I've always been awkward, I guess. Always nervous being in public and groups and stuff. And now, it's so much worse." I don't know what to say, and before I take the time to formulate the words, I feel them rising up and pouring out. "I always feel like I am on edge, waiting for someone, some guy, to jump out at me or something. I get scared in the shower, even though it's just girls in there, and it's all individual little shower stalls. I figure someone can see me or something. Even changing in my own room. I know that no one can see. I know that I'm fine going back and forth to class, and walking down my own hallway. But I also knew that I could drink at a bar, and I was wrong about that, so I guess I just don't know."

He reaches across the table and takes my hand in his. It's

familiar, but friendly, not romantic.

"I don't know why I'm telling you this. I should be doing nothing but thanking you. Nothing even really happened to me. It could have, I know, and probably would have if you hadn't been there." I pause, willing the flow of words to stop, but they pour out anyway. "I just feel so... so... so damned vulnerable. And I hate that. I already feel so out of place and stupid and just like a big lump, and now it's so much worse. I'm like an egg or something. I can crack so freaking easy, and I am funny-shaped and I don't fit anywhere..." I trail off. Oh my god. Why did I say all of that? Why? I pull my hand away, waiting for laughter or some awkward response. *Oh, well, good luck with that. Look at the time! It's getting late. Sorry you're crazy.*

I can feel his eyes on me, the heat in my cheeks, the proximity of his hand that he hasn't moved yet.

He clears his throat. "Danielle." His voice is solid, though quiet. "I want you to listen to me very carefully. You don't have to believe a single thing I say. But I haven't lied to anyone that I can remember, and I don't think I'll start now. Nod if you're listening."

I don't look up, but I nod.

"Okay. You are *not* an egg. You are a beautiful - don't interrupt - a beautiful young woman that something really shitty happened to. It didn't *almost* happen. It happened. More almost happened, but something did still happen. You felt safe, and then you weren't. That sucks. And it's okay to know it sucks. But you know enough of the world to know there are so many people in it. Not everyone is going to be comforting and caring like I saw your friend be that night, but not everyone is going to be a piece of trash like that guy who was putting that stuff into your drink."

At the mention of Christine, guilt sweeps over me again, but I push it from my mind. Best to think of it later.

"It's just..." I can't find the words. My throat is thick, my hammering heart attempting to leap out of it. I try again. "It's just, I just know that he's still out there. What could he have been charged with? I never had to give a testimony or anything. I kept waiting for police to show up to interview me, take a statement, like they do in all those cop shows. Nothing. He would've had a little talking to, a slap on the wrists, and then he'd have been free to go."

"I don't know anything about that. But we have to assume that if that was the case, he would have been scared enough to never try it again. And besides, I don't think he would come after you."

"I don't think so either. But he is not exactly alone, is he? How many others have tried stuff like that? How many have gotten away with it?" My voice drops to a whisper, and I fight to keep the tremor out of it. "How many have gotten away with worse?"

He doesn't say anything, just takes my hand again, and holds it while his tea and my coffee get cold.

CHAPTER 6

Danielle, age 20
2000

Christine says if there ever is an appropriate time to eat ice cream straight from the container, this is it. Hell, it's tradition! So last night we sat cross-legged on her bed, watched a bunch of chick flicks on my parents' small hand-me-down TV - I fell asleep sometime during the fourth one - and I cried a bit, and this morning I feel better.

We broke up a couple days ago, but I didn't cry about it or even tell Christine about it until last night. That's when she ran out of the room to get the ice cream and a stack of DVDs she had rented just for the occasion. "Real sappy ones, too," she assured me, and ordered me to get into my PJs. "You can't properly eat ice cream out of a bucket while crying at cliché sad movies, unless you're wearing PJs."

I always knew Christine was confident, and pretty, and just awesome, but now I know she is smart, too.

So I wallowed, and today I am focused, still sad, but okay.

We had only dated a few months, after all. And it was super casual that whole first month. The age gap was a little weird, but I think it affected him more than me. After all, his students were only a little younger than him, and he always said thinking about that made him really uncomfortable.

Plus we are at totally different places in life. Even when I had called that first night, to go for coffee back when I was still too scared to leave my room, he had been sitting in a meeting with a couple coworkers, going over some specific curriculum or something. I was taking tests, and he was marking them, and while that didn't seem a problem to me - he wasn't *my* teacher after all - he was a lot more concerned. What would the parents of his kids say? I reminded him that they weren't actually *his* kids, but he just would say I didn't really understand it. He never said that with anger or anything, to be fair, more just as a statement of fact. And he was right; I didn't understand that fuss. Still don't.

I did know that he didn't stay away from me, though. At first I thought it was out of pity or some odd sense of obligation, but it didn't take me long to realize he really did care about me, he really did find me interesting and even *beautiful*.

He even told me I was talented, and when he took me to an art show sometime during month two, he whispered to me that some day something I did would be in a place like this. You know the ridiculous old movies, a couple of which I just watched last night, when the woman puts her hand to her forehead and faints? She swoons? Yeah, it took everything I had in me not to do that. Though of course I didn't believe what he thought of my future, part of me wondered. He was so smart. Maybe he was right.

We disagreed once in a while, but always about silly things, about movies or where to go to dinner, and it never even became an argument, let alone a fight. He was generally right, anyway, but he never held that over me or made me feel stupid or anything.

But the physical part of it, well, that was where it got complicated. The first time was sometime in month two, just a bit after my birthday. We were at his apartment - a real nice apartment, too, that wasn't all hand-me-downs and cast-offs - and I knew what was going to happen that night. I had prepared myself, worn a low-cut top, tight black pants, and new lacy underwear, a matched set. I wasn't happy with how I looked, but after turning this way and that in the mirror, inspecting everything both before and after I got dressed, I decided it was as good as it was going to get.

He made me dinner, and we shared a bottle of wine. Stuffed chicken breasts, and homemade pasta. I didn't even know you could make pasta at home, but he did it. The food was delicious, of course - way better than I could cook. Hell, better than my mother could cook. But then, everything he did was perfect. Christine says that was because I was wearing "new relationship rose-coloured glasses." I just figured she was jealous that I had a real, mature, serious man spending time with me and cooking for me and pouring me wine, while her boyfriend chugged beer with his buddies and used his skateboard as his primary mode of transportation.

After dinner he opened another bottle of wine, and as he poured us each another glass, then another, the volume and intensity in his voice increased. Soon I could hardly hear the strings of the instrumental "mood music" CD he'd put on after dinner.

"It's just amazing, you know, when the kid, the kid who has driven me crazy all semester, when he finally *gets it*, it's like you can almost see the light bulb go off, and you just think, huh. I actually taught something." He paused, lifted the glass to his lips and took a deep drink. "I just worry it is the ultimate form of narcissism or something. That high you get - yeah it is a total high - from knowing that you maybe helped the kid figure something out. That realization, that's because of you. It's freaking awesome."

"I bet you are an amazing teacher. I bet everyone loves you." I swung my legs up, so they were bent beside me on the couch, which forced me to lean closer to him.

"Nah, I mean, some kids like me, sure, but not everyone. No way." He leaned back and looked at me. "But you...." He trailed off.

"Yes? What?" The wine made me feel warm.

"You're something, you know that? Seriously. You are so damned sexy. I wish I didn't think you were beautiful, but you are. And so talented."

"Talented? Nah. I could never do what you do."

"No." He shook his head. "No, you couldn't. Or maybe you could. I don't know. But that isn't what I mean." His voice was different with a little alcohol in it. It was lilting, and deep, and even as he looked up at the ceiling, I was drawn closer to him. "If you could do anything, anything at all, in this whole world, what would you do? Pretend that money is no object; education, training, experience: none of it matters. What would you do?"

I looked at my glass. I had never told anyone before. "Travel photographer," I blurted. I rushed to get it all out before I changed my mind. "I want to see the world, see the people and the places in it, and I want to take pictures that make people think about it."

He looked at me then, really looked, and the intensity lurking there sent a shiver through my limbs. I didn't know whether to look away or lean in closer. "That's amazing, Danielle." He used my full name. No childish, boyish "Danny" here now; Only sophisticated "Danielle" who drinks wine on her boyfriend's couch, who will one day take photographs of the whole world.

"You know what?" He set his glass down, and I did the same, and then he was kissing me, and my hands were around his neck, and then we were in his bedroom, and it did not occur to me until much, much later to wonder at the answer to that question of "what".

*   *   *

47

In the end it was the age thing that was just too much. Even that first morning after, he couldn't quite meet my eyes, and I couldn't help but feel I had done something terribly wrong, despite all of his protestations that I hadn't. He swore he just felt so guilty. I was so young, after all, my whole life ahead of me, and while he was far from elderly, he had done the whole college experience, and he didn't want me to miss out on any of the "fun".

"Oh yeah, real fun," I rolled my eyes. "Except when you put your drink down for a minute." And then he looked at me, and took me again in his arms.

But the day we broke up, we were in public, and there wasn't the chance to get him to take me in his arms. No matter how I pressed into him, he wasn't going to relent, and I knew it was happening long before it actually did.

One minute we were talking about the end of my semester, and my plans for the summer, and the next he had gone pale, and was stammering about "holding me back" and "interrupting my youth". I told him then he was being condescending, and it was my choice, and then he asked me what my parents would think about bringing home someone his age. I told him that I didn't care too much about what my parents thought one way or another, and then he thought that maybe I was only with him as some form of rebellion against my parents. When I pointed out that generally people only rebel if they are angry or something, and I said I didn't care, not that I was angry, he got quiet.

"We are just in very different places in life right now."

"So you've mentioned. Numerous times."

"I just don't see how it's going to work, Danny." *Danny.* That got his point across. Though he had called me it before, it had always seemed affectionate or endearing. This time it was the same voice he used when talking to his brother, or that I imagined he used talking to his students.

"You know what? Fine. If you want to insist on thinking you are some old man, then that is fine by me. You go and sit in your rocking chair and talk about your precious work and do whatever else old men do, and I'll go and see the world and actually live life. You want to act like you are some saint or something, giving something up because you are just so god-damned decent? Okay. I'll let you have that one. But I'm not some child." My voice dropped. "Please don't just think I'm some child." My powerful exit speech was crumbling. I lifted my chin, determined to leave with some dignity. "I'm done. I didn't really know if I loved you anyway." I turned and left, crossing my fingers, begging the universe to make him call me back.

He didn't.

CHAPTER 7

Mark, age 29
2002

Twenty-nine isn't old. I know that. I also know I am one of only a handful of friends unmarried. Hell, most have kids by now.

Not that I am anxious for any of that. I mean, sure one day I definitely want kids, but I also deal with them enough day-to-day. It's more the place in life. I thought I'd have it figured out by thirty, and while I have the work life running along okay, the rest of it, not so much.

And that is what I am thinking about as I hold the phone in one hand, the business card in the other.

I glance around my apartment. I remember another evening here, a dinner I made for her, a bottle of wine too many, a conversation. It was some of the best sex I had ever had, which made me feel so much more guilty. I wanted to not like it. I wanted to not like her. But I did.

It was okay, then, after we broke up. Ending it was, of course, the right thing to do. We'd only dated three months or so, after all, and while it shook me up, there was no irreparable damage done. I was sure everyone was better off. I dated a bit, off and on, and then Darlene had come along. Darling Darlene. We met at a teachers' conference, through a friend of a friend. She taught the second grade, was upbeat and so sweet it did not seem real at first. But no, she was real. Darlene was in my life for almost eight months. She even met my parents. I thought about the future with her. Vacations, together, evenings on the couch, holidays... But I couldn't quite get that picture in my head to focus. It was always fuzzy, always lousy reception. It just wasn't right, and that came out during one of our many arguments towards the end.

"Are you even happy?" I had asked her.

"Not really," she answered. Her hands on her hips, defiant, yet her eyes were sorrowful.

"Then what the hell are we even doing?"

And that was that. Though we hadn't officially been living together, she had stuff here, and I boxed it up and dropped it at her place, where she had a similar box waiting. Of course both were labelled with names and contents. I'm surprised we hadn't also each put a sticker on our respective box with a smiley face and some words of encouragement.

That was a month or so ago, and I have been more or less content living the bachelor life since then.

This afternoon, though, I saw *her*. Danielle. How was it fair that such a brief interlude with that girl two years ago left me so shaken?

She was window shopping, facing a clothing store window, wearing a black coat. The particular shade took me back to the first night we met. This jacket was full of zips and buttons though, not a slinky number like her dress had been.

I was coming out of the book store, turned, and stopped short when I saw her. Her hair hung down, straight, and I could see a pink sweater peeking out from under the open jacket. Her blue jeans ended on a pair of black platforms, and she looked so much like a vision that only the cheesiness of that word - "vision" - brought me to my senses.

I debated turning back and hiding in the store until she passed by, sure she wouldn't want to see me, and then of course while I was debating, she turned and settled her gaze on me.

"Mark?"

Her voice in that one word was even more subdued than I remembered, but I had memorized every lilt and cadence of the way my name fell from her lips, and that was still the same.

"Hi Danielle."

God, why did she have to smile like that? She was going to be upset; that's okay. Yes, time had passed - a lot of time - but there was no doubt bitterness there. After all, she stormed out. Yes, I'd been breaking up with her, and yes, it was the right thing to do, but she didn't even look back.

Would she rail against me now? Yell? She had never yelled at me before. Perhaps now it was time. Or would there just be disdain, dismissal? Or maybe she had forgotten everything altogether; everything except, evidently, my name. Why did she have to smile like that?

"How've you been?"

She kept her smile, searching my face and - did I notice? - my left hand? Well, enough time had passed. I guess it was a fair assumption.

"Oh, I'm alright. Work, you know. You?"

"Can't complain. Especially with everything going on now." She gestured around her.

A few months ago, I'd woken up to the news of the attacks in New York. We couldn't turn on the TV without seeing the coverage. It was all my students could talk about. Though our main street in our smallish Canadian city would likely never know that level of devastation, it still had left us all, well, me anyway, pretty stunned. I spent more time than I cared to admit wondering at the brevity of life and the pointlessness of so much that seems so necessary.

"I know what you mean." A somber pause before I continued. "But what are you up to now? I'm kind of surprised you aren't even down there, taking your photographs."

"Oh," she blushed, and I realized, too late, that I had somehow erred. "I don't really do that now."

"Take pictures?" I knew it wasn't my place to pry, but I'd seen her work, and I always thought that it was something she was passionate about.

"No, I still do that. But more for, like, friends; engagements and birthdays and stuff. Just in my spare time. I am working around here, actually. Couple blocks over. Macallens?" It was the name of a little store that sold artsy clothes and artisan jewellery.

I tried to keep the dismay from my face. Needless to say, it was not what I pictured for the girl who I knew had the talent to take the world in her hands and shape it - no, capture it - through the lens of her camera.

"It's not my dream job or anything, but it pays the bills, and it gives me enough so I can do the photography stuff on my own time."

I reminded myself it was none of my business what she did. But it comforted me, for some reason, knowing she was still taking pictures.

"Actually," she went on. "I don't know if you remember her, but my roommate from college? Christine? I'm going to shoot her wedding in the spring."

"That's pretty cool," I said, and meant it, though I did think that Christine seemed a little young to be getting married.

"Anyway, I should probably get going." She sounded flustered. No wonder, with an old flame from years ago prying into her personal life.

"Yeah, me too."

"Oh!" she exclaimed, reaching into her purse. She pulled out a business card and a pen, and I watched, dumbfounded, as she flipped over the card and wrote her number. "The first time we met, you gave me your number," she smiled as she handed me the Macallens' card. "This time, I'll give you mine."

I'm sure my mouth dropped open a bit, but I took the card

and put it in my pocket as she hurried down the street, tugging her purse up further on her shoulder.

And now here I stand, my eyes taking inventory of my own apartment, still holding that card. Do I dial the number? What could I be getting myself into? What could happen? I turn to the bedroom. Yes, sex, likely. And if it was anything like I remembered, good sex.

More than that, though, if there was sex, then there would be someone here in the morning. Someone to sit at that table - I looked at the kitchen - and drink coffee, while I made her breakfast. I wonder if she still likes her eggs over-easy? And maybe at that table, or here, on this couch, there would be conversation, although probably of the awkward variety, and these walls could actually hear a woman's laughter again.

On the other hand, there could be expectations; a relationship, even. Well, what exactly was wrong with that? She wasn't nineteen anymore. But could there be trust and romance and even a future where there had once been heartache? Yes, even though the relationship had been short, I wasn't ashamed to say that it had broken my heart to break hers. It was the look in her face that did me in, that, "I didn't really even know if I loved you anyway," with the voice quivering, tears clinging to the corners of her eyes. It killed me. It took everything in me to watch her walk away and not call her back, take her in my arms, and dry those eyes.

But who would have known if it would have even worked out a month or two more? She was young, and I was, well, younger than I am now. Hell, she is still young. Is it reckless to re-establish contact? Even just for a friendly drink? Do I even really want to?

I gingerly place the phone down in the cradle and walk out of the room, determined to leave well enough alone.

Maybe only ten minutes pass before I stalk back in, grab the phone, and hover my hand over the little buttons that would connect me to her. I had stared at the card long enough to have her number memorized. Why should I call? Hell, why

shouldn't I?
   I dial.

CHAPTER 8

Danielle, age 22
2003

The appointment is for one o'clock, but I was hoping my mother and Christine were willing to meet for lunch before that. I hadn't seen Christine in awhile, not since before the holidays, and I was anxious to hear all about her first Christmas as a "Mrs." Plus, if I'm honest, I really wanted to gush about wedding plans, and I hoped my enthusiasm might make my mother a little excited.

Mom said she couldn't do lunch, but Christine and I went anyway.

"Well," Christine said, after we caught up a bit and I explained my mother would not be joining us until the store, "at least she agreed to come shopping with you. That's something."

"Yeah, it's just... I don't know. I always thought of the whole mother-daughter wedding dress shopping thing as one of those moments. Damn media, setting up unrealistic expectations."

"One of 'those moments'?" Christine asked around a

mouthful of sandwich.

"You know, a cheesy perfect moment. Like, I try on a dress and she dabs at her eyes and realizes how much time has passed and her little girl is all grown up. She tells me I look like a princess and we hug. That kind of thing."

"You watch too many movies."

I chuckled. "Yeah. Pretty dumb, right? I guess when you think of it, this whole wedding thing is kind of dumb. Not the wedding itself, but, like, the dress and the shoes and the centerpieces and whatever. All that stuff doesn't really matter. I know that. Deep down, I know that, but I still kind of like the planning."

"I hated it." Christine shook her head. "I remember getting into a fight about our first dance song. We actually were screaming at each other about that. Wedding planning makes normal people insane. What's the biggest fight you guys had so far about it?"

I stabbed at my salad. "We actually haven't had a big fight."

"That's lucky. Not fighting about wedding planning. Smart to not get crazy about all of that."

"No, I mean, we actually have never had a big fight."

"No?" Christine's sandwich was halfway back up to her mouth. "Like, about anything? You guys argue and stuff though, right?"

"Not really. I mean, we don't always agree on everything, but it's never like, an argument."

Christine's BLT was threatening to fall apart if it didn't make its way either to her mouth or her plate soon.

"Why?" I asked. "Is that weird?"

"I guess. I mean, no. I don't know." A tomato landed on the plate. "I don't think it's super common."

"Do you think it's bad?"

"I wouldn't say that." She set down the rest of her sandwich. "It's better than, like, screaming at each other all the time. About first songs, for instance." She picked up the errant tomato and smiled.

"I don't want to fight with him or anything. Sometimes I just wonder. Like, is there actually passion there if we don't feel strongly enough to get mad at each other?"

"Or maybe you just figure stuff out before the fighting starts." She tilted her head and raised her eyebrows. "I'm telling you, too many movies." Christine shoved the tomato in her mouth, her momentary surprise forgotten.

"It does sound a little crazy, doesn't it? 'I want to fight with my fiancé.'"

"Little bit. On the plus side, you're normal. I did tell you that normal people go crazy because of wedding planning."

I stuck my tongue out at her. "On a different note, how cool is it that I get to say 'my fiancé'?"

"Soon, you'll be saying, 'my husband.'"

I blinked. "Wow. I guess you're right, but that just seems…" I shook my head to clear away the overwhelming sense of, well, everything that rushed at me right then. "I'm going to be someone's wife. Huh."

"Oh don't start getting all emotional and life-contemplative now. It's going to be a long day with enough opportunities for that. Pace yourself, girl."

*****

In the end, we did find the dress I would be wearing to walk down the aisle. I do have to acknowledge that my mom she showed up, which was just a little more surprising than I would care to admit out loud.

At the first store we tried, I pretended not to hear the saleslady talking to Christine and my mother while I was in the change room.

"I don't know if she will find anything in here."

"Well, she's just started looking," Christine answered her. "Even if we get a few ideas, she might be able to give it some thought find something later."

"It's not her decisiveness that is the problem," the saleslady said. "The bride-to-be won't fit into our sample gowns."

There was a gasping, gulping, sobbing sound that I realized

came from my own throat. I tried to swallow it down, but it got stuck somewhere in my throat. I tried again, backing against the wall, staring at my grotesque figure in the mirror. I winced at the sight of me. *A beautiful bride? Me? Who was I kidding?*

I determined to stay in the change room the rest of the day.

That's when I heard my mother's voice, without a trace of emotion. "Of course she won't." *Gee, thanks, Mom.*

I was so busy trying to fight the wave of nausea that swept through me I almost didn't hear her continue. "She won't fit anything here. She isn't a prepubescent boy."

Christine snorted in an attempt to cover her loud burst of laughter.

"My daughter is aware of what size she is. She is also aware that you order in dresses and therefore that you do not actually expect the ones hanging here in your tiny store to fit her. I am also aware that, while some girls who come in here will fit into these gowns, far more won't. That is why you are carrying those pins on you. So how about you just worry about bringing her the dresses she wants to consider, and let her worry about her sizing herself."

"But ma'am -"

"If there is an issue with ordering a size in a particular gown that she wants to see, simply don't bring her that one dress. But I'm going to wager that most can be ordered to fit girls much bigger than her. So I will thank you to keep your underhanded comments and opinions to yourself and bring us another dress."

Behind the door, where I was safe from being seen or heard, I was left with the overwhelming urge to weep. My racing heart slowed as I gulped in breath after breath of stale, lavender-scented air. The wall was cool behind the back of my head, steadying and calming me.

I only half-listened to the saleslady mumble an apology and hurry off, only somewhat heard Christine laugh and congratulate my mother on her bad-assness. I brushed at my eyes as I turned this way and that, taking in my reflection in the mirrors in front of me. Mom was right; I had known I would be pinned into each dress here to get an idea of shape and style, and if I loved one I would order it. I hadn't expected to fit into all of the dresses. I also knew I wasn't small, but I hadn't thought, truly thought, that I was that big.

Yet, more than all those expectations that I did or did not have, the most surprising thing of all was hearing the words that my mother spoke when she didn't think I could hear her.

The world tilted a little. I was surprised that the door didn't swing open, that when I eventually did hesitantly come out of the change room, everything seemed so normal. My mother was still there, flipping through a magazine. Christine was still there, eyes moving over all of the dresses on display. How was everything just as it had been when I closed myself within that tiny room? Maybe I didn't know all the things I thought I did. If I could be so wrong in my assumptions about my own mother, what the hell did I know about anything?

We didn't buy my dress at that store. We found it at the second. When I asked the saleslady if I would fit some of the sample dresses, the quizzical expression on her face was almost comical. "Of course," she said, handing me a ribbon. "Any you want to try, Hun, just drape this ribbon over. And here." She handed some to Christine and my mother. "If you see any you would like to see her in, you do the same. Take your time. This is supposed to be fun."

No bells went off when I found the dress. No fireworks, no invisible orchestra. To be fair, none of that happened when I fell in love with Mark either; just a slow smile spreading across my face. I felt it before I even looked in the mirror and saw myself grinning like a five-year-old being given her choice of candy.

Though I was far from confident, the sting of insult and offense from earlier was lessened by knowing I probably wasn't repulsive in this dress. I reminded myself that Mark had asked me to marry him; he knew who I was and he knew what

I looked like. He would love me in whatever I wore down the aisle.

Christine and my mother both approved, and that was that. I wanted Mark to love me in this lace and ribbon and silk. I wanted him to look past the size that the woman at the store thought so inconvenient and I thought so offensive. To clarify: her attitude didn't offend me as much as the inconvenience my size caused her. My offensiveness offended me. I should be livid at her attitude, at the audacity of her speaking about me like that to my best friend and mother. But I wasn't. And I further annoyed myself by not reacting the way I should have.

"You like the dress?" my mother asks as we blink at the brightness of the outside world. The sun had shifted since we parked, and now, returning to our cars, it was directly in front of us, blinding.

"I hope so. I just paid for it."

"Just making sure. It's not the dress, you know, that makes a good marriage. Of course it's also good to like the dress."

"I know, Mom."

"I had a gorgeous dress."

"I have seen the pictures. It was lovely."

"Old and dated, now."

"Yes, but still lovely."

"I have a hard time remembering the girl who wore that dress. I was young, you know. Even younger than you."

"People change over time." I am hesitant. Wonder of wonders: Is my mother actually opening up to me? Will we get a cheesy perfect moment after all?

"I guess I'm just saying, make sure you know what you are doing with this whole wedding thing."

"The whole wedding thing?" I hate to parrot her.

"The marriage, I mean. Not just the wedding."

So much for the cheesy perfect moment.

"Mom, I know not everything is sunshine and rainbows when you get married. Everything isn't sunshine and rainbows when you are single, either."

"It's just, you're so young…"

"I know how old I am. I know how old he is. I know things get tough sometimes."

"It seems you sure know a lot."

How long has it been since that same voice was telling me, as a child, that I knew nothing? It feels like mere moments ago, though I know years have passed. How long has it been since that same voice was standing up for me, making me question everything I thought I knew? It feels like it had never happened at all, though only hours ago I was standing there, listening.

"I don't know everything, but I do know that you and Dad aren't happy." *I can't ever remember you being happy*, I add inside my head.

My mother's lips pull into a thin line.

Before I can stop the words from flying out of my mouth, they are free, flying and whipping between us. "I'm sure you want the best for me, but I also know that I'm not you, or Dad, and Mark isn't either. Just because things are turning out one way for you doesn't mean they'll turn out the same way for me."

I am aware of Christine just in the corner of my peripheral vision, fiddling with her purse strap and averting her eyes from the scene developing in front of her. Having Christine witness this embarrasses me further. I remember my parents' house, the screaming, the slamming doors, that broken picture frame. And me, hiding and avoiding and wishing it all away.

My mother's face turns hard. She nods once, but says nothing.

I wait, looking at her, also saying nothing.

Christine continues to avert her eyes. My mother and I stand, face to face, her hands dropped to her sides, her back straight. I realize my own back is straight, my own hands are at my sides, and I'm reminded of the drama games we played in school. *Mirror, mirror, Simon Says.*

After an uncomfortable silence that stretches on enough for

me to be aware of the breeze blowing the hair on my arms, Christine at least coughs in a quiet way that seems to attempt to remind me of myself.

"Look, Mom…" I trail off, hoping now she will say something. Nope. *Okay then.* "I appreciate that you are probably just looking out for me. I didn't mean to insult you."

"You have a lot to learn, Danielle." Her low voice is just above a whisper, and beneath the anger there is a layer of hurt that is almost palpable. She opens her car door and stares at me over it.

Today had been going so well. She had even stood up for me. She had been there at one of the few times that I didn't feel like a sausage stuffed into its casing. She had laughed with us, joked with us, even been on the precipice of opening up to me. What had I done?

"I'm sorry, Mom."

Another single nod, but her expression doesn't change. "I have a long drive, Danielle. I should get on the road. I'm glad you found your dress."

"Mom -"

"It's fine." She cuts me off and slides behind the wheel before I can continue. Why had I ruined the day? Why did I have to be so stupid? So useless?

CHAPTER 9

Mark, age 30
2003

I don't know why she hasn't put away the suitcase yet. She bought it just for the honeymoon, and other than the wheels on the bottom, it still looks new, sitting open on the bed. She already unpacked everything. She ran every piece of clothing through the laundry before folding, every sleeve bent at a perfect angle, every pair of pants creased with precision, every one of her dresses hung on hangers spaced at exact distances. She even vacuumed up the sand that had hitched a ride home in the corners of the suitcase. Yet the case itself she left, open now, waiting.

Though she'd moved in most of her belongings before the wedding, she herself hadn't technically lived here. When she did move in, I expected more to change, but so far she's keeping her belongings put away, most of them even out of sight. So much for the bras and nylons I expected to be draped over every surface in my bathroom. So much for the makeup I expected to be strewn over the counters. Instead she appears determined to take up as little space as possible. Walking into my apartment now, save for the new wedding photograph hanging on the wall, one could hardly tell a woman even lives here.

Perhaps that's why I noticed the suitcase in the first place. Everything else being put away, this stands out all the more. She is gone now, running errands, printing honeymoon photographs for the album she bought months ago, the pages ready for each smiling, posed face.

Everything was just as planned, going back to the wedding itself. Girls go crazy for all that wedding stuff - ceremony and flowers and all that. I just wanted to get married. So I let Danielle plan what she wanted for the wedding, and I showed up and brought the ring with me and said what I was supposed to say and kissed when we were supposed to kiss and gave the speech I was supposed to give and smiled for the camera when I was supposed to smile and danced when I was supposed to dance. If I'm honest, it wasn't as bad as I thought. Hell, it was kind of fun. But I was looking forward to the honeymoon. A week on a beach in Mexico sounded awesome, and it was. Danielle was beautiful all done up at the wedding, but if I am being honest, it was nicer to see her at the airport, checking and rechecking our passports, mentally itemizing every item in her carry-on, fiddling with the band on her left hand, and grinning at me when she saw me watching her. It was nicer to see her looking like herself. And it was definitely nicer to see her in that new swimsuit she bought. I know Christine was the one who'd talked her into the white bikini; Danielle is way too self-conscious for it to have been her idea.

Of course, she spent so much time behind the camera that we probably did not get many shots of her in that bikini. And even if I do vaguely remember snapping one or two, I highly doubt those are the ones that will be making it into that honeymoon photo album. Shame - I'd love to see that again.

I'm reminded of teaching my students personification as I look again at this suitcase. The hair on my arms stands up, unnerved by the way the suitcase seems to stare at me. What is it about suitcases, lying there empty? Before a trip, they are full of uneasy anticipation. After, they are almost regretful, longing to go back to those unfamiliar hotel rooms, those airport carousels. Nothing symbolizes discontent like an empty suitcase. Or perhaps an undeveloped roll of film.

I'm disappointed in myself for thinking of work earlier today. Shouldn't I be thinking of being married, not of the planning and marking I will need to catch up on come Monday? "The old ball and chain" - that's how all the guys have been referring to her in the months leading up to that Saturday in that church. I laughed and joked and wondered. What would they say if they knew how quiet she was, how unassuming, how little she resembled any iron object, let alone a restraint? She's more like… huh. I am not sure what she is like.

I suppose it isn't a bad thing to not be able to objectify your wife. God, that word: wife. Now *that* is surreal.

That thought propels me to the kitchen, where I open a cupboard, searching for a glass. She has even started unpacking the things we got for the wedding. When did she do that? How did she manage to do all this so quickly? I take down one of the highball glasses we registered for, and pour myself a whiskey.

Well, I wanted it, and I got it. The wedding and the wife and the whole thing. No more waiting, neither uneasy anticipation, nor regretful longing. And here I am now, someone's husband. That someone is just trying to make me as comfortable as possible. I'm sure that's why she hasn't swept through here, leaving pieces of herself on every freestanding piece of furniture. She's so considerate. And it's not like I want my apartment covered in girl stuff. I'm sure her presence felt more as time goes on. It's only been a few days, after all. I wander through the apartment, from room to room, sipping at the amber liquid swirling around the ice cubes. Before I am half-done my drink, I am standing back in the doorway of the bedroom, watching the empty suitcase, the only out-of-place thing in here.

I'm not sure whether to be unnerved by it, or comforted.

CHAPTER 10

Danielle, age 24
2005

Mark is at the school late tonight, coaching basketball, I think. Some sport or activity, anyway. He told me not to bother making supper, but of course I did anyway. The only thing worse than being tired after being around teenagers all day is also being hungry. So I fixed him some tomato soup, which I have warming on the stove, and a turkey bacon sandwich, which I have covered and waiting in the fridge. I just want him comfortable and content, because I want to talk to him about something specific tonight, no matter how late it is.

It's two years ago last spring we exchanged our vows, and now that we moved into our own house, I finally feel ready to have a talk about the future. Specifically, if children will be joining it soon.

Even before the wedding, Mark always said things like "when we have kids" and "our kids". Now, the new house is organized and Mark's career is solid. I don't know what else we could be waiting for, what hesitation there may be, why we haven't started trying, or at least talking about it.

I plan to remedy that, and soon, which is why I'm practically pacing the kitchen floor when I hear his car pull into the driveway.

"How was it?" I call to him as I hear him remove his shoes and coat.

"Oh, you know. Same old. The boys are looking stronger but they have a hell of a lot of work to do before this weekend." He walks to me and kisses me on the cheek. "I said you didn't have to make supper, remember?" He tilts his chin at the soup simmering away on the stove.

"Nonsense. It's nothing fancy."

"Did you wait for me to eat?"

"Of course."

He gives me a funny expression, then shakes his head. "You didn't need to do that."

"I know."

He moves to the table, dropping his work bag onto it with a thud. "Well, can't say I don't appreciate it. It's just that I have a lot of marking to do yet, and I don't think you really want to sit around and watch me do that."

"Anything I can help with?" In my mind I'm seeing our own child sitting at that table, paper and crayons strewn everywhere, creating pictures that eventually will be displayed on the refrigerator, as proud as any art in any gallery.

"Not really. Paragraph responses. Thanks, though."

I move to the cupboard, taking out a bowl. After ladling the soup out, I sprinkle pepper on top of it before placing it, and a spoon, in front of his regular seat. Then I go to the fridge, take out the plate with the sandwich and a cold beer. After placing these down as well, he looks at me, genuine warmth crinkling up the corners of his eyes. "You're too good to me."

I laugh, dish out my own soup, and join him. "I just want you to be happy. I know how tired you've been lately."

"Ah, it's that time of year. Between the basketball season and the new semester and getting stuff organized for midterms, these few months are nuts."

"And after that are finals and all those year-end events," I remind him. "You're always busy."

"Just part of the job, Sweetie."

"Maybe someone else could take over basketball?"

"Season's over half done. No point in that."

"Maybe next year then?" I'm picturing him pushing a stroller, not staying at the school coaching someone else's kids on the basketball court.

"I doubt it. Who would do it? Besides, I kind of like it. Gives me another way to see those kids, you know?" He lifted a spoonful of the soup to his mouth, blowing on it a bit before slurping. After he had swallowed, he continued. "Why all this talk about me quitting coaching?"

The man just gave me a flashing neon "welcome" sign.

"Well," I begin, repeating the lines I had rehearsed in my mind so many times today. "I was thinking. We are all unpacked and settled in the new house now."

"Yeah, you were awesome at that. Thanks so much."

"And your job is pretty secure."

He dunks his sandwich into his soup. "Pretty much. I mean, nothing is ever guaranteed. And that's the thing." He bites off the corner of his sandwich, soggy from the broth. "Part of what makes my job pretty secure is all the coaching and other stuff." He says, the words finding their way out from around the bit of bread rolling around in his mouth. "If you aren't willing to coach and organize and sit on committees, well, you may as well get your resume ready." Another dunk into the soup.

"Okay." I am not thrown off at all. "So we have the house. And your job is awesome. So what are we missing?" I smile, waiting.

He raises his eyebrows in my general direction. "We're missing something?"

"A baby!" I didn't mean to squeal.

He puts down the sandwich slowly. He eyes flick across my expression, down my body as far as he can see while I am sitting at this table, and back up to my face. I realize he is searching.

"Danielle, are you….?"

Oh. "No, no, I'm not pregnant," I rush, waving my hand a little as though shaking my head wasn't clear enough.

"Okay. I'm confused."

"I just think it's high time we started trying for a baby."

"Trying?"

"Yeah. So I've decided to stop taking the pill."

Each nod of his head seemed to take a full minute. "I guess it makes sense to start thinking about it. I don't know though…" he trailed off, shifting his gaze to each cupboard door, each item on the wall of the kitchen.

"You don't know? What's wrong?"

"It's just -"

"Just?"

"I kind of always thought you would want to travel more or something first. You know, for your pictures."

Damn it. This again.

I take a deep breath that I hope is not too audible. "We've been over this." My spoon makes its way around my own bowl, but it doesn't move any of the soup up to my mouth. I haven't eaten a bite yet.

"I know, I know. You're just so talented -"

"No I'm not."

"Danielle…"

"Mark. I think it is sweet that you think I have this great hidden talent, but the truth is, I'm really not that good. I tried once."

"You never -"

"Yes, I did. Right after college, I got a whole portfolio done. I even applied to a couple magazines that send people out to take pictures. I never heard back from them."

"Why didn't you tell me?" His mouth is open a little, his eyes definitely on me now. I don't like it.

"I didn't tell anyone."

"Danielle, stuff like that, they say that you have to go through a lot of rejections before you ever make it."

"Save it." I sigh. "I'm not one of your students who needs a pep talk. It sucked, okay? Checking my phone, my mail, my email, every day for weeks and then months. And not a thing. I'm not spending my whole life doing that." My spoon clangs on the rim of the bowl, my hand settling onto my lap. "If I was something special, it would have happened. But it didn't. And I really don't want to talk about it ever again."

His head tilted at me, the inside corners of his eyebrows pulled together and raised. "I'm sorry you got hurt, Honey."

"I said I don't want to talk about it." My voice is quiet to keep the emotions that are threatening to bubble up, under the surface where they belong.

The pause that follows may be the only thing in the house pregnant at the moment, but I haven't given up my goal for the night just yet. As I look at Mark, I can almost see the soup before him cooling, almost see the thoughts whirling in his head, full of potential possibilities and problems. He is the realist; I know that. If I was a gambler, I would bet that he was calculating costs and years and making plans.

"Your soup is getting cold," I point out, breaking the silence.

"It's fine. And I can heat it up if need be."

"Let me do that," I jump up, reaching for his bowl.

"Sit down, Danielle."

I sit.

"Here's how I see it."

In his pause I can see him weighing each word on his tongue before allowing it life. His lips press together, his brows pull in. *He'll get wrinkles that way*, I think.

"These things take time," he continues at last. "Sometimes six months. Sometimes more."

"Oh I know that."

"And if we do this, our lives will never be the same. Anything you ever wanted to do, well, it will be a lot harder."

"I know that too. You aren't the only one who has been around kids before, you know."

"The kids I'm around can drive and go on dates. And neither of us has been around babies a lot."

"I've babysat!"

"Not exactly the same thing, Danny." The indulgent tone when he uses that name - Danny - prickles, but I don't reply. I don't want this topic to be closed tonight just because I can't control my temper.

"Okay," I say through gritted teeth.

"And I have to be honest. I really don't like that you never told me about your portfolio."

"It wasn't any of your business."

"It almost feels like you were hiding something from me."

"I wasn't hiding -"

"I know that you don't feel like it," he cut me off. "But you still were."

The nerve of that man! That part of my life, that waiting by the phone, checking the mail, shelling out every cent I had to make and send away that portfolio, all of that happened before he and I got back together. Maybe if he hadn't dumped me in the first place, we never would have been apart and then he would have seen all that. Instead of hurling my indignation across the table at him, I bite my tongue. Literally.

"And there is also the fact that you are still very young," he is saying. Always the age thing.

"But, if you really think you are ready, and we are ready, and if you really want to..." he reaches across the table, his palm out, and I blink and move my own hand from my lap into his.

"Are you saying....?" Neither of us is finishing our sentences. I am afraid of it, afraid that he will change his mind.

"Yeah, I guess so. We can try."

I jump up and run around the table, my soup completely forgotten as I throw my arms around him, kissing him over and over again, on his cheek, mouth, forehead, even his eyes.

He is laughing, only pretending to resist, and this moment, this moment right here, is one of those ones that I will know will weave itself into the fabric of our relationship and myself, one of those moments I will come back to, again and again, for the rest of my life.

CHAPTER 11

Mark, age 32
2005

I'm still reeling from the last discussion we had about this whole thing. I don't know why Danielle insists on making decisions as though we already have a baby. She isn't even pregnant, and already I catch her standing in the doorway of the guest room, and I just know that she is planning where to put the crib and the change table and whatever else a baby needs. All in a matching color scheme, too.

The last one was about names. She has a list already. Sure, right now it contains just about every name in existence, but there it is, penned in her precise script in a notebook, with lines that have been meticulously drawn, separating the "Boy" heading from the "Girl". I'm a little surprised that the left list isn't in blue ink, and the right isn't in pink. I hope she never finds out I thought that, or she will no doubt redo the whole damn thing.

I just don't understand how she can be so focused on this thing that hasn't even happened yet. What is so god-awful about our life now that she is so anxious to change it so drastically? Her rose-coloured glasses are so focused on these "somedays" that she is ignoring all the day-to-day things that make our lives, our lives.

What does make my life mine? Mostly, her and work I guess. So if she isn't happy, if she wants our lives to change in such a drastic way, what does that leave me? Am I just reduced to where I am now, sitting at my desk at work, a stack of marking in front of me, waiting for the next parent complaint, the next staff meeting, the next detention supervision? What the hell am I doing?

Shit. When I drink too much coffee I guess I get introspective and a little melancholic. I can't handle my caffeine anymore.

"Hey, Mark. Still here, huh?"

I glance up. It's Allison, a woman who comes in and coaches girls' volleyball. Junior Division, I think. I can't remember anything else about her, except that it's her first year here, and she seems nice enough, even though I've only nodded at her a couple of times.

"Yeah." I gesture at the stack of pages I'm hiding behind. "I am not making much progress though."

"The end not in sight yet?"

"Never."

We exchange a few pleasantries about the day - which kid did what, a little general gossip about our coworkers. Then she gets to the point.

"A few of us are heading for a couple drinks. You want to ditch the marking and come along?"

In the staring contest between the stack of papers and myself, I'm losing.

I consider accepting the invitation. "Nah. The wife's probably waiting for me. I can put off going home if I'm working, but probably shouldn't if I'm hanging out with people."

"You're putting off going home?"

Did I really say that? I glance up sharply, and see her head tilted a little, her black, shining hair swinging slightly from the movement.

"I didn't mean it like that."

"Of course not." The right corner of her mouth lifts a little.

"I was just joking."

"I get that. It's fine."

"No, I don't want you to think that I don't like my home or my life or something."

"Mark." She lifts her hand up as she says my name, palm facing me. "I said it's cool. I get it. I'm not prying. You don't have to explain."

I wait, tapping my red pen against my leg.

She waits, standing there beside the "25 Grammar Mistakes to Avoid" poster. The potential for serious awkwardness is thick. If I keep talking, I'm going to make it worse. I don't want a coworker judging my home life, but I don't exactly know how to proceed without blundering.

"So you're not in for drinks, right?"

I smile my thanks at her for diffusing this. "Yeah. Thanks, but no thanks. Next time maybe."

"For sure. No pressure. I'll tell the others you're busy." She gives a little half-wave as she sweeps out of the room. "Happy marking!" she calls over her shoulder.

Putting off going home. Where did those words even come from? I'm not putting off going home. I love my house. We finally bought our own place a few months ago, and we are all moved in and it is actually feeling like home. Why would I avoid that? And I'm certainly not avoiding Danielle. I love that woman. Sure, she's sometimes so curled up within herself I wonder what she's thinking. Other times she blasts it at me with a megaphone.

The imagination that lurks within her, though… no wonder she's so quiet so often. I wish I had the creativity and talent she has. Not just with her photographs, but with everything. I watch her sometimes, when she doesn't realize it. I see the way that she looks at the world. It's beautiful.

I took her to an art gallery when we were visiting Toronto

last winter. We wandered through the rooms and halls. It was fine, but not really my thing. I liked some of the newer things well enough - abstracts and whatnot. But she loved it all. At one point I found that she wasn't in the room with me anymore. I moved to the next exhibit, then the next, and then just when a feeling of annoyance started to creep up my neck, stiffening the short hairs there into fine points, I saw her in the corner. The sight of her actually made me stop short and catch my breath.

Her back was to me, but I would know that denim jacket anywhere, the shape of her back, the way her black skirt hung a little past her knees, the way her red scarf fell off her shoulders, the incline of her head. A few tendrils of hair had escaped from her ponytail, and I was overwhelmed by the desire to tuck those strands behind her ears and feel the skin of her cheek against my fingers.

She had the gallery pamphlet in her hand, which was drawn into her chest, as though she was placing it over her heart. Someone brushed passed me and I realized I was gawking, and not at the art. At least, not at the art on the walls. But I was standing very near the entrance to the room, and seemed to be in the way of the other patrons. I took a few steps toward towards her corner, quietly, not wanting to disturb her thoughts.

She was staring at a painting. I can't even remember what it was now, looking back. I would have only given it a cursory glance, but there she was, clearly enthralled. She was chewing almost imperceptibly on her lip, her eyes moving across the canvas in front of her. As I drew closer I could see her eyebrows drawn up, her breath forcing her chest up and out, up and out. She was fixated. What could she see in that painting? What enthralled her so much that her breath heaved from her like that? I wish I saw the world that way.

How could I be avoiding a woman like that? Sure, right now she is the woman who is focused on nursery plans and charting dates on a calendar, but she is also still the woman who I couldn't take my eyes off of as she stared at that painting, who smiled so self-consciously when I finally cleared my throat to alert her of my presence. She is still the woman who makes me coffee every morning, with a teaspoon of sugar on weekdays and a shot of liquor on weekends. She is still the woman who cries at sappy movies, who brings home crazy jewellery from her job, shrugging and explaining that at least she is supporting local artisans. She is still the woman who threw herself across the table at me the night I told her we could try. That crazy, passionate, sexy photographer.... She's still there, too. I'm not avoiding.

I clearly misspoke. Something slipped out that I didn't mean, that I didn't even feel. I am sure Allison didn't think any less of me. And that pity I read in her large, brown eyes when the corner of her mouth gave that slight lift, well, I must have imagined that.

A glance at the clock shows that almost ten minutes have passed since I even looked at a paper. I'm wasting my time here. Marking bag in hand, I throw in the rest of the short stories. I may as well stare at them in the comfort of my home - which I am definitely not avoiding. If I didn't want to go home, I would have gone for drinks with Allison and whoever else, right?

Right.

By the time I get home, Danielle has dinner made. *Of course she does.*

"Just a pasta thing," she tells me. She's leafing through a magazine, and even from the quick glance I throw it as I pass I can see the word "fertility" on it. *Good grief.*

I go to the kitchen and grab a beer, then move back to the living room, where I sit across from her and spread my marking out in front of me.

"You don't want supper?"

"Not yet. I want to get a few more done." I shuffle the stack of papers onto my desk and fish out a red pen from the recesses of the bag.

"You didn't finish at work?"

"I never finish. You know that."

She smiles. "If you ask me, if you didn't assign it, you wouldn't have to mark it."

"I didn't ask you." I'm not sure, between the two of us, who is more surprised by the snap at her.

She blinks. "Sorry," she says. She looks down at the glossy pages in her hands a moment before flipping them closed. She clears her throat, pausing, and with a more cheerful tone of voice that calls to mind a thick layer of cupcake frosting, she continues. "What are you working on tonight?"

"Just some short stories. Grade eleven." I lean back, a paper still in my hand. I sigh. "I didn't mean to snap at you. Guess I'm just tired. Or frustrated. Or something."

"About me?"

"Not really. More about work, I think."

"You think? You don't know? So it could be me?"

Shit. "It's just work."

Hell, it could have been true. Tonight, for example, I was supposed to be marking fantasy short stories. So far I had read twelve stories about dragons, three about unicorns, one clear rip-off from a recent film, and something that read more like a video game manual. A cursory glance at the paper on the top did not reassure me. John had written a story about himself wearing wings, flying around the world, comic-book style.

So yeah, it was fair to say that I was frustrated with work.

"Do you want to talk about it?"

"Nah. Like you said, I do it to myself. I'll just get a few more of these done, and then we can have dinner."

"Want to curl up and watch some TV after dinner?" Danielle has put the magazine down and is leaning towards me so the front of her shirt dips down, offering me a clear view of her cleavage. She shifts a little as she does, moving her hand towards my knee with a coy smile. I know what she's doing.

"Maybe." I turn my knee away so she can't reach me.

"Maybe?"

"Let me guess. It's the right day of the month, right?" I hate myself a little for the condescension I hear in my words.

"What?" She draws back.

"You know what I said, Danielle. I'm not a machine or a circus animal."

"A circus animal? What?"

"I don't perform on command." I stand up.

"No. That's not what I meant." She's blinking, rapidly. In another circumstance she'd almost be batting her eyes. "That's not why. Please sit back down."

Now that I was standing, I had no idea why. What was I going to do? Storm off? To where? Why? Because my wife wanted to have sex with me? Jesus, something was wrong with me.

I sit back down, but can't keep the glower off my face. I don't look at her.

"I'm sorry. I just… I mean…" I can tell by her halted speech that she's struggling to find the words.

"It's fine."

"Clearly it's not. I just don't understand…" Trailing off again.

"Forget it, Danielle. I'm just tired. Like I said before." I hate the way the words are clipped. Hate the way each one drips and splats across the floor. But I did tell her, didn't I? I told her I was tired. *Why couldn't she just listen?*

It wasn't that long ago that we never fought. I can't even remember the cause of our first argument, but I remember that it was messy, and long, and loud. Maybe not fighting for so long makes our arguments harsher.

I refuse to look at her. She's probably crying, She cries for every reason, and I am just not in the mood to wipe away tears tonight. That's right. The woman I love is no doubt crying, and I don't want to see it, because then I will obligated to comfort her, and I just don't feel like it. Further proof that something is wrong with me.

"Okay." Her voice shudders. *Yep. Crying.* "I'll leave you to the marking. Let me know when you're ready for supper." She gets up then and leaves the room. It hardly even occurs to me to wonder where she went.

CHAPTER 12

Danielle, age 25
2006

I don't know where I am. The last thing I remember is being surrounded by a lot of people, swaying to the music. Feeling faint. Falling.

But that wasn't me, now.

That was a younger version of me.

My heart is slowing, the room coming into focus. I race to grasp the remnants of the nightmare before it all slips from me, blown away by Mark's snores.

There was a bar. A loud, crowded bar. A band was playing. Rock. No, that's not quite right. Punk rock.

There was a girl. She was me, a younger me, exactly the same face I saw in the mirror every morning, yet prettier than I ever realized at the time.

There was a boy. Except he was putting something in her drink. In my drink.

I knew he was there, knew what he was doing, only I couldn't turn around, couldn't confront him, couldn't stop my hand from reaching out and grasping the glass, couldn't not swallow the burning liquid as it splashed into my mouth.

That's not how it happened in reality, though. In reality, someone had stopped me from drinking that drink, swallowing the powdery, dissolved contents of that pill. Someone had stepped in, stepped forward, and days later, weeks, maybe, that same someone had taken me out for coffee.

My dream didn't care about reality, though.

In my dream, that someone wasn't there.

Mark wasn't there.

CHAPTER 13

Mark, age 35
2008

It was raining the night he died. I'd only taught Riley one semester, but I had his brother, John, in his last two years of school. With basketball season coming up, I'd expected to see Riley more. He'd really grown up and was probably going to go out for the team this year. I mean, he would have.

There was an announcement Tuesday morning, before classes started. "All staff members, please come to the staffroom immediately." That's never a good sign, but there is no way any of us could have predicted this. We came in, cracking jokes about donuts, holding coffee cups and binders. Our principal was standing by the table in the middle of the room, and as she saw us, she leaned forward, averting her eyes, clinging to the chair in front of her so hard that her knuckles turned white. The contrast with the dark green fabric, pilled and ragged, was striking.

She didn't need to tell us to be quiet. I had never seen her looking like this, and I doubted any of my coworkers had, either.

She cleared her throat as I shifted from one foot to another. I didn't know what she was going to say, but I knew I wouldn't like it.

"Last night…" She paused, cleared her throat, and went on. "Last night, Riley Cowan died in a car accident."

Time stopped. Somewhere near me, someone gasped.

"Some of you might remember his brother, John, who went to school here a couple years ago. He was driving Riley. I guess he was in town visiting from college, and they went out for dinner or something… We don't know everything. Riley's aunt called us this morning to tell us. I guess the road was wet -"

"It was raining." Someone stated the obvious from across the room.

"Yes. It was raining, and another car skidded out coming towards them. She said John swerved to avoid them, but he was going a little fast, and he lost control. They hit a lamppost. John's banged up. A few broken bones, but he'll be okay. But Riley… Riley wasn't wearing his seatbelt."

"Oh God." I was only vaguely aware of the murmurs around me, reaching out to me from somewhere far away. I should have been able to pick out the owners of those voices. I'd worked with them for years. But it was all in a fog. Maybe even a downpour. The kind of downpour that made it impossible to tell the voices of people you had known for years, or see a car losing control in front of you.

"There will be an announcement later today, and we will have grief counsellors on hand." She went on about the policies in place, about his friends, whether or not he had a girlfriend, who we should watch out for extra carefully.

I thought of Riley, an athletic kid, lanky, sitting in the far right row in my classroom, all angles and sarcasm. His hair was a little longer than fashionable, his clothes a little baggier, but not so much you would notice unless you saw him every day. I tried to think of the kids who would be most affected, who to watch for more than usual signs of grief (as though the word *usual* fit at all). His friends, obviously. The other boys about his age who would be questioning their own mortality. I tried to picture a girlfriend, but couldn't.

And oh god, poor John. He'd be just - what would it be now, twenty? - just twenty-years-old, who now has to live with being behind the wheel the night his brother died. Not his fault, of course, from the sounds of it. But I remembered the twelfth-grader, the kid who had a bit of an attitude, but when it came "crunch time", always did what he had to do. His name even brings to mind a night at home, when I was upset over something else, and read something of his - an essay, maybe? A story? Something that was creative but just really bothered me one particular night. Something about flying.

Yes, John. We would worry about him, and their parents, and friends, but who was going to worry about us? We spent more time with that kid, that awkward, sarcastic, funny kid, than anyone else who wasn't family. Hell, maybe even more than family. I read his thoughts that he scrawled across countless pages, knew the way he looked at books and poems and movies and the world. And now.

Jesus Christ.

Now, *just like that*, it was all gone.

It's Thursday now, and the shock hasn't really worn off. The initial, stunned reaction has, I suppose, but now it's more raw. Now it hurts. Now I see the desk he used to sit in, and I just… I want the numbness back.

He had green eyes, right? I think they were green. Why can't I remember for sure?

That kid. He was just a kid. It was so stupid. Such a waste.

"Mark?" I'm not sure if it's the first time she's said my name, but it's the first time it registers.

"Allison?" I look towards the door, towards the voice. I'm standing in the middle of my room, staring at his old desk.

"You okay?" Her voice is timid. A pause. "Sorry. That's a stupid question."

I don't say anything for a while, and she comes into the room, leaning against my own desk near the front. It's quiet, but not the kind that is uncomfortable.

"Allison?" I repeat.

"Yeah?"

"What colour were his eyes?"

"What?"

"Riley."

"I know who you mean."

"What colour were his eyes? Do you know?"

I can feel her eyes on me, but they aren't judging. Or maybe they are, and I just don't care. "I'm not entirely sure. I didn't really know him. Only met him a few times. But, something tells me green, I think."

"We spend every day with these kids. We stare at them and talk to them and listen to them and coach them and care about them. But I can't…"

I close my eyes, and the desk is crashing sideways and onto the floor before I am aware that it is my hand that has pushed it. Books left by a forgetful student fly across the room. I am saying something - yelling it maybe - and I don't know what it is, but am pretty sure it's not school-appropriate.

I slam my hand down, and it meets another desk. I slam it again and again, hoping to somehow make the desk take this feeling, this awful, overwhelming feeling, out of me. Let it travel through my arm out onto this desk.

I don't know how many times I slam it, but it doesn't help. That desk, too, gets shoved across the room. That's the thing about having an emotional breakdown - because even I'm aware enough to know that is what's going on here - in a classroom. Plenty of desks to throw around.

I shove another, and then another, until all the desks around me are toppled, shoved, even thrown, haphazardly scattered wherever they land.

I could stomp through the rest of the room, ripping down posters, heaving the desks even more. Hell, I could put a hole in the wall. But I don't feel better now, and I don't think any of that would help either. Instead, I collapse to my knees, as though I were praying, as though I had ever done anything remotely resembling that.

Seconds pass, then minutes. Eventually I come to my senses enough to hear heels click the few steps towards me.

Allison.

I had forgotten she was even here.

And then she is beside me, lowering herself to the ground, a hand on my shoulder.

I raise my puffy, red face to look at her. "I'm sorry. I shouldn't have done that." I'm as embarrassed by the crack in my voice as I am of the tears that I know are clinging to my cheeks.

"It's okay," she says, turning her attention away from me toward the door. I see that she closed it at some point during my rage. I'm still surprised no one has come knocking, but since classes let out an hour or so ago, I guess the school would be a little deserted.

I'm also more than a little annoyed at myself for being so concerned about being heard.

"I don't usually lose it like that. About anything. But this is just all so - "

"I know."

We're both staring straight ahead now, as though we were actually reading the "parts of speech" posters under the board at the front of the room.

"It's a shit thing," she says, and I like that she doesn't mince words. "That's all there is to it."

"Yeah."

And there, in the center of my classroom, in a space created by my grief-driven abuse of desks and chairs, Allison reaches over, and takes my hand.

"It'll be okay," she says. "It doesn't feel like it, and I can't tell you how, but it will be okay." She slowly gets to her feet, bringing my hand up with her. "Now come on," she is saying, pulling on me. "We both need a drink."

CHAPTER 14

Danielle, age 32
2013

"**H**ow's it going, Danny?" Calvin's voice on the phone sounds a little distracted, but then again, I talk to him so rarely that it is possible this is just his regular voice and I don't remember it.

"Oh I'm fine. You?"

"Pretty good. Work and all that. Same old." Oh yes, my brother, the businessman. I am still not really sure exactly what his job entails, but I do know that it has something to do with advertising. "How's work for you?"

What else can I say? "Fine." I manage a local clothing store that also sells artisan jewellery. I live in a small house, in a small town, with a yard and three bedrooms for two people. He lives in a two-bedroom loft in the middle of the city, with his girlfriend and pet cat. Our lives are a little different. I could hardly complain to him about the system that crashed last week, or a coworker who always calls in sick Fridays and Saturdays, or the customer who insists on buying five or more full outfits, then returning all of them two days later.

"Yeah? You busy at the store?"

"Sometimes. It's okay."

"Doing the photography thing still?" *The photography thing.* I move the phone away so he can't hear me sigh.

"Yeah, sometimes. I've done a couple birthdays recently." I don't tell him that they were kids' birthdays. I don't tell him how hard that was, seeing those faces, hearing the peals of laughter as the older ones chased one another around, the giggles that were more like gurgles as the one-year-old smashed the cake right into her face. I don't tell him how it hurt my heart to smile and chat as I captured those moments. I don't tell him that I pulled my car away from that house, only to park it again a block away, bawling into my steering wheel.

"That's awesome. Any other photo shoots?"

"Some. Basically whatever someone is willing to pay me for. Family photos, engagements, even a wedding once in a while."

"Yeah?"

"Yeah. You know that." What's he fishing for here?

"I'm glad you still do those too. Wondering if you wanted to come up and do some photos for Shantelle and me. Some engagement ones."

"What?! Really?! Engagement ones?!" The excitement is sincere. "Congratulations!"

He tells me about the proposal itself when I ask, and I can't help but smile and think of my own. More than ten years have gone by since Mark slid out of the booth of the coffee shop where he first took me, so many years ago, back when I was still in college, back when I was too scared to leave my own dorm room. He got down on one knee there, on that dirty floor, and asked me, and I didn't even answer before throwing my arms around him, tackling him backwards as everyone around us clapped and whistled and congratulated.

I'm so happy for Calvin; I truly am. Shantelle will be good for him, and he'll be good for her. She's one of those girls that you wish you could hate, because she is pretty and has a good job and is always stylish and volunteers too, of course. But as much as you may want to, you can't hate her because she's also one of the gosh-darned nicest people alive. They'll be happy together, I know. I can just tell about these things, and I say as much to Calvin.

"Thanks, Sis," he laughs.

"I mean it."

"I know. But seriously, we want you to come up for a weekend. You tell us when. Shantelle specifically requested an afternoon of manicures or something for you two. We can do dinners out. You know we have the guest room. And then you can take some engagement photos for us."

"I haven't done much work in the city before. I'm sure the light and stuff is different. Shadows from the buildings and whatnot…" The excuse sounds lame, even to my own ears.

"Well thank goodness you'll be here a whole weekend to figure all that stuff out." *So much for that.* "I know it's report card time for Mark, so he's probably busy, but he's invited too."

Mark. My eyes move around the empty living room.

"No, you're right. I'll ask, but he's pretty busy."

"So just a weekend with my big sister then. Unless, of course, you don't think Mark can stand me taking you away from him for a whole weekend?"

I try to remember the last time we spent an entire evening together, let alone a whole weekend.

"I'm sure it will be fine," I say.

"He'll just have to cope, huh?"

"Right," I say. *Yeah right*, I think. He probably won't even notice when I'm gone. "He's been busy lately," I explain. "He's working on his Master's, you know."

"Oh yeah, he said something like that last Christmas. How's that going?"

"Good. It just means he's gone a lot. He's still working full-time, and he was really busy even before doing this whole thing."

"Is it good for his job? Getting his Master's?"

"Definitely. Like, in the long term. Now it's kind of tough. Between the regular planning and marking and coaching, and now his homework and classes and stuff…and he hasn't really been the same since that student of his died."

"Well that would mess anyone up."

"For sure. Of course." I tried to balance on the line between propriety and confession. I needed someone to talk to. "I tried to be there for him. Still do. But it's been years now, and he's just… I don't know. Guess it's a guy thing."

"Yeah, might be. Do you still talk to Christine?"

"Sometimes, on Facebook and stuff. She's got the kids, and that makes things tough. She's busy."

"Everyone's busy, Danny."

"Yeah." My eyes land on the photo of Mark and me, hanging on the wall, from our trip to Toronto, years ago now. We're a little off-center. It's one of the few candids I actually display in the house, taken courtesy of a self-timer and solid ledge. You can't even tell that we're on vacation in the image, but we are, and you can't tell that we'd spent hours right before that picture was taken wandering through an art gallery, but we had. You can, though, see me smiling at the camera, mid-laugh, eyes almost closed. And you can see him looking at me, grinning at my reaction to what he had whispered in my ear. His arm is around me, and I'm leaning into him. When was the last time we were that comfortable together?

"My point is," Calvin is saying, "You should talk to her. Message or email or send a messenger pigeon or whatever you old folks do. Smoke signals, maybe?"

"Very funny. Those mere two years between us means I'm wiser."

"Oldie."

"Respect your elders." I'm laughing now. This is why I talk to my brother much more often than either of my parents, as rare as that still is. He listens, but he also makes me laugh.

After I return the conversation to wedding plans and get a

few possible dates for the engagement shoot, we hang up. I busy myself around the house, finishing up some dishes, putting away some laundry. It doesn't take long, though, to find myself back in front of that photo, swearing to it and myself and anyone else that may be listening, that I would get *that* back from wherever it disappeared.

*　*　*

I am in bed, pretending to read and not check the clock, when Mark finally comes home.

"Hey, Hun. You up?" He walks past the open bedroom door without looking in. "Yeah," I call after him. After he doesn't respond, I continue. "Just reading."

"Okay." He comes back to the doorway then, his smile easy. "Anything good?"

"Another classic." I show him the cover, and he nods.

"I'm going to jump in the shower. I hit the gym after study group. I probably stink."

I raise myself up onto my elbows, offering a shy smile and allowing the blanket to slide down enough that he can see what I'm wearing beneath the blanket, which isn't much. "I'm sure you don't stink."

His eyes travel over as much of me as I can see, and he arches his eyebrow slightly, his mouth in a straight line. "Yeah. I do." He doesn't say anything else, just pulls his t-shirt off and tosses it into the hamper across the room.

"You sure you don't want to just come to bed?" I am trying for seductive, but even I can hear the unspoken plea behind the words.

"I'm sure." There is no trace of hesitation or consideration before he leaves the room, and it is only a matter of seconds before I hear the shower turn on down the hall.

I lower myself back onto my pillow. *It doesn't mean anything,* I tell myself. Maybe he really did just need a shower. It's not like I'm always in the mood after I come home from the gym. Plus he's probably tired, after work and then studying and then working out. *No, it definitely doesn't mean anything.* If I tell this to myself enough, perhaps that little nagging voice in the back of my head, hidden behind the echoes of all my thoughts, will shut the hell up.

I pretend to be sleeping when Mark comes back into the room. I feel his weight settle into bed beside me, smell the shampoo from his towel-dried hair, hear his deep, even breathing, and wonder at how this man, less than an arm's length away from me, is somehow so far away..

CHAPTER 15

Mark, age 41
2014

Danielle is off for the weekend, helping Shantelle, Calvin's fiancé, with some wedding stuff. I would be lying if I said I wasn't relieved that she was gone. Not that I don't like having her around, it just makes my life a little easier to not have to tiptoe into the house late at night, or jump in the shower every time she wants to have sex, or comb through my texts, leaving only the most innocuous messages.

I'd never bring Allison here. That's not why I'm glad I'm home alone this weekend. My home is off-limits, as is hers. She knows about Danielle, of course. She knew about her before any of this started, before I even remember talking to her. But she is not welcome in our home. I could never bring her into the space and the bed I share with my wife.

That doesn't make this - any of this - okay. I know that. There is no way to excuse what I am doing, not even to myself. When it started, a few years ago now, it was all I could think of all the time. Every time I saw Danielle, the guilt bore through my gut, ripping apart my heart and tempting me to confess everything.

I know people in these situations always use banalities like "It just happened." I would say that, but I don't lie.

Or, at least, I didn't.

No, I knew what I was doing. My decision-making skills maybe had been impaired that first time, but I still knew what every look meant, every "accidental" brush of her hand, every joke that was just on the edge of vulgar. I knew that the way she angled herself towards me didn't just mean that she was interested in my thoughts on standardized testing. And when her hand rested on top of my knee, I didn't pull away. I should have, but I didn't. I knew that there would be that hesitation at the end of the night, that final chance to play innocent. I knew I didn't have to follow her to the motel the next town over, that I didn't have to fall into that cliché. I had so many chances to back out, to just go home, to my wife. But my choice was made the minute I didn't move away from her first touch, there in my classroom, amid thrown desks and scattered books.

Immediately, and for days after, I was sick. Literally sick, throwing up, the self-hatred eating away at my insides. I swore to myself it would never happen again.

But it did. Months later, it did.

And then it did again.

After a few months, I stopped pretending to myself that I was still a good person. I tried to keep up the facade for everyone else, but I knew the truth. I didn't want to embarrass Danielle, of course, but sometimes I wished she would find out. I wanted her to scream at me, throw something, even hit me. I deserved it.

I still do.

About the same time I stopped pretending to myself that I was a decent human being, we also started actually planning our meetings. We always say that - we have a meeting. It makes it difficult when, on my less guilt-ridden days, there is a staff meeting at school. She raises her eyebrows at me when she sees me head into the staffroom then, after the announcement reminder for staff, and I have to hide the smile behind my hand, so when I sit down I can attempt to look thoughtful at whatever presentation is going in the front of the room.

The months have passed, and the guilt dulled quicker than I care to admit. We avoid each other at work, exchanging only the most casual of conversations, always directly related to school. But every few weeks, one of us invariably sends the other a message about a meeting, and there we are, conducting our illicit rendezvous in motel rooms, her friend's cabin, even the backseat of a car once or twice.

She is unmarried, and dates occasionally, but nothing has lasted so far. I'm not entirely sure how I feel about that.

When I asked her about it once, her status as a single, she shoved me playfully on the arm. Her short blonde hair curled at the ends, and I tucked it behind her ears. A whisper somewhere in the recesses of my mind almost wondered at the memory of watching my wife at a gallery and wanting to do the same to her, but that whisper fell silent.

Allison was spread beneath me in bed, my elbow pressed down beside her, my hand supporting my cheek, looking down at her while I traced her stomach with my fingers. "Don't be dumb," she said offhandedly. "It's not a good look on you."

"No, I'm serious. How come you're single? I don't get it."

She shrugged. "Don't know. Just never really worried about it the way the rest of my friends did, I guess."

"It's not too late."

"I'm not exactly worried about it now either."

"Did you ever come close?"

"To getting married?"

"Sure."

"Yeah. Once. Got the ring and everything,"

"What happened?"

I could see the muscles in her shoulders as they again rose and fell. "He didn't really like me I guess. He expected me to stop being me. I wasn't okay with that. So we split up."

My fingertips moved from her stomach to her hip. I love that she allows herself to be seen naked with the lights on.

"Tell me more."

"Not much to tell. We fought a lot. One day the fight was about what I would and would not be allowed to do once we were married. I didn't deal too well with that."

"No, I don't imagine you would." Not this girl, with fire only thinly veiled in her eyes. Then she smirked, and her arm encircled my neck, pulling me to her, and that ended the conversation.

*   *   *

That was more than a year ago, and now, with Danielle gone, I am heading out of town as well. After I casually mentioned my "bachelor weekend" to the guys in the staffroom, Allison dropped by my class, under the pretense of asking about a particular student.

"I'm heading out of town, too," she said. "Weekend away. With a friend." That pointed qualifier - *with a friend* - was just shy of obvious.

She told me where and when she would be there, and I knew I would be packing my bags, just the same as I knew what her hand on my knee meant that first night.

I am going through the house, making sure everything is fine for me to leave for a couple days. I take a plate out of the cupboard, a knife from a drawer, and the jar of peanut butter from the pantry. The knife goes straight in the jar, and when I pull it out I carefully scrape it against the side, then leave it and the plate on the counter. Next I head to the recycling, and grab a few empty beer bottles, scattering them throughout the house. One can in front of the TV, by the game controller I also strategically leave out. One can on my desk in the office. The rest on the kitchen counter. *Good.* I take a tea-towel from the rack, bunch it up, and toss it on the counter as well. Next I move to the bedroom, where I take out some clothes - sweats, a t-shirt, socks - and throw them on the floor. In the bathroom, I take the toilet paper roll off the holder, and flip it around. I always replace the toilet paper facing the way opposite of the way Danielle replaces it. The towel on the rack is removed, and then rehung, entirely askew. One more walk through the house and I could almost congratulate myself on how convincing it all looks, if I wasn't so disgusted.

Now that all of that is taken care of, I can actually pack my bag and go. I throw clean jeans on the bed, a button-down shirt, a sweater, underwear, socks, t-shirts. I am picturing room service in bed, and wondering why I am bothering to pack so much clothing when I have little intention of wearing any of it, when I realize that I have no idea where Danielle keeps the overnight and carry-on bags. I know where the big suitcases are - those would be impossible to miss - but the smaller bags aren't with them.

I tour through each logical place, crossing them off one by one. Finally I come to her closet. I am rummaging past a basket full of workout clothes, a shoebox containing the heels she wore to walk down the aisle - I set those aside quickly - when I come to a nondescript box shoved near the back.

Six years ago, I wouldn't have snooped. But now, since I know the kind of person I am, I have no problem allowing my curiosity to get the better of me. Compared to everything else I have done to Danielle, opening a random box doesn't seem significant, especially considering my reason for being in her closet in the first place was to find a bag to pack my stuff for a weekend away with my mistress. I hardly even hesitate.

I really should have.

There is a blanket on top. It is yellow and soft, with a satin edging. It isn't new; in fact, it clearly was loved so dearly once upon a time that it has been worn right through in places. I finger the satin and wonder at the little fingers that once did the same. Some of the edging has been mended, and I see the tiny, lopsided stitches. Someone small once loved this blanket, and someone once loved that someone small. And somehow,

Danielle ended up with it. Maybe it had even been hers.

The blanket covers the rest of the contents of the box. I'm not sure if it was intended to hide or protect it all. Probably both.

There are two books, both the boardbook style, designed for chubby little fingers or for late night reading by parents. One is titled "For My Daughter", and the other is "For My Son". It's then that I realize what this box is, what she meant for it to be.

With the books, there are onesies, most of them homemade, with clever and witty sayings, artistic designs, and references to inside jokes. Danielle made these, I realize, pulling each one out of the box and inspecting it before attempting to refold it back up with the same care she had. When did she do this? How many hours were spent planning and dreaming and creating? How many times did she bend over the dyes, cut out the stencils, imagine the little kicking and squealing and wiggling person who would wear them?

Oh god. How many of those times were while I was with Allison?

There are ten altogether. Ten little onesies, in almost every colour. Under the onesies is a collection of nursery rhymes, vintage, and clearly from a second-hand store. Had Danielle gone shopping for this book particularly, or had she stumbled upon it looking for some lamp or something? The book found its place among the rest of the menagerie on the bed, and I pull out the final item - a pair of little, crocheted socks. Danielle doesn't even crochet.

Had she packed all of this up immediately after that last trip home from the hospital? Had she found a box in those first few days back home, sobbed through packing up each item? Had she thrown everything in and shoved at all away to save herself the pain of seeing these things, or had she deliberated on each item? Had she pulled these socks to her chest? Had she cried over these onesies? Or had her face been set in a stony determination, focused on each task to help her get through every action?

Until this point in time, I hadn't even known Danielle had been collecting these items. Had she started before, when we first started trying? Or even before that? Or had these items been picked up and created after she got that positive result? So many questions flitted around me. I could almost see them in the air, escaped from the box with each item unpacked.

Why had she never said anything to me? I knew she cried, when we found out. I had held her when the doctor told us, only half listening to his reassurances. She was still young enough. The important thing was to get that first positive. She hadn't done anything wrong. The human body has ways of knowing when something isn't okay. This one, this time, it just wasn't viable. On and on, the words hung empty in the air, all of those "right things" to say, none of which actually felt right.

The feeling when I was half-listening to all of that, with Danielle pressed into my shoulder, shuddering and gasping through her heartache, is coming back to me now, looking at all of this, spread out over the bed we laughed in. The same bed we tried... and then succeeded...

The memories are lodged in my throat, and a part of me wonders if you can choke on something that isn't physically there. Can you choke on hurt?

It only takes a matter of minutes to put everything back. I shift the books so they are side by side. She had both, because she wanted to wait and be surprised. So like her. Instead of waiting to buy one book, she got all excited. She stood in a store, all glowing and thrilled, imagining us snuggled up, reading books to an infant. Boy or girl? We didn't know, so she bought both.

And now here they sit, under a faded yellow blanket, buried in a box, hidden in the recesses of a closet.

I seal the box, and put it back in the furthest corner, carefully arranging her dresses so they hang neatly in front of it. The basket of workout clothes is next, and I make the effort of standing back to inspect my handiwork, to make sure everything is as it was before. I would rather have Danielle suspect the existence of Allison than have her know I went through that box.

The space at the top of the closet, where she normally keeps her suitcase, first purchased for our honeymoon, is empty now. Of course she took it with her to visit Calvin and Shantelle. The void accuses me, of so much more than infidelity.

Back in the kitchen, I grab a beer and my phone. I have a few calls to make, and the first is to Allison, to attempt to explain why I won't be joining her this weekend after all.

CHAPTER 16

Danielle, age 33
2014

This is the morning I leave him.

I knew it was today as soon as I opened my eyes. I have been waiting to choose the perfect day, trusting that when the time was right, something would somehow tell me. Some sign from a higher power, a change in atmospheric pressure, perhaps. Perhaps I would be sitting there, and a feeling would wash over me, complete calm or overwhelming certainty. Maybe a lightning strike would hit me while I was drinking my second cup of coffee.

But it wasn't that. I opened my eyes this morning and the first thing I saw was the back of my husband's head, his hair, unwashed since yesterday morning, dark and a little long. There was nothing particularly remarkable on this morning about his hair, but I studied the way it curled at the base of his neck as if I was seeing it for the first time. How often did I wake up to him lying next to me? It was sporadic, that much I knew.

What bothered me the most, though, was not that he wasn't always there when I woke up. It's that his lack of presence wasn't odd enough to stand out. I honestly could not remember when he was or wasn't there. I just didn't notice anymore.

So I knew I couldn't stay.

What was keeping me here anyway? There are the practical concerns, of course, but I have enough money to get by for a bit, and I can stay with friends, or even go out to Calvin's if need be.

No, I'm the one who put the big pause button hovering over my head. My thoughts, worries, feelings. The connection and love I feel, and wish I didn't.

There are memories hanging on the walls of this home that I once unpacked and organized and decorated, but the last memory I framed and hung was years ago. No new memories were being made, no new pictures taken, no new inside jokes or whispers between us in the night.

Wandering through the house now, towards our bedroom, I trail my fingers along that last framed image. The marks left behind tattle-tale how long it has been since I bothered to dust. There was a time when I took such care in this house, when I folded each item of laundry and kept each surface clear of every empty tea cup and dust particle. When did I stop making an effort? When did I stop caring? Was it the same time he stopped crawling into bed with me at the same time every night? Maybe it was before that, when he stopped bringing home the piles of marking, stopped curling up on the couch with his glass of scotch, alternating between laughing and cursing while he read essays and stories and whatever else. He used to read me snippets of the best lines and the worst, and I would come and stand by him from wherever I was in the house, shaking my head or nodding solemnly or giggling along, as source material dictated.

When that stopped, was that when I stopped caring?

Or was it after that? Was it when I noticed the same name

pop up on his phone again and again? Or, worse, was it the morning I held that phone in my hand as he showered, resisting the urge to type in his password, that urge to snoop through the messages I just knew were hiding behind the bouncing yellow envelope?

I wanted to go through that phone. I didn't do it, but I wanted to. What would it have solved? If I found something, my suspicions would have been confirmed, and I'd have felt worse. If I didn't find anything, there would be some other horrible, inexplicable reason for these changes, and I'd still feel worse.

But I still picked up that damned phone. I still thought about it.

It weighed in my hand like an anvil in a child's cartoon. The coyote holds it, pauses, looks at the audience in shock, and proceeds to plummet through the sky and the trees and the ground, leaving behind only a coyote-shaped hole. That phone pulled me, and when I looked down, I almost expected to see a heart-shaped hole in the ground at my feet.

I wanted to skulk through his messages, his images, his history.

So I had to leave.

My suitcase, previously hidden behind out-of-season boxes of shoes and clothes, now yawns across my bed - our bed - waiting. Clothes are pulled from the closet, rolled and folded into neat piles, each item fit into each empty space, until the suitcase's mouth was filled. It takes less time than I thought it would, and before I know it, I'm standing once more in the center of our living room, looking around me. What else should I take? Do I take that last picture of us smiling at the camera? Photo albums and scrapbooks? Gifts he once bought me, back when we still bought each other gifts? How do I cram so many years into only a few boxes and bags?

I know I don't need to take everything now. I know I can come back for "the rest", whatever that may include. These books, those old CDs, this stack of movies, the art on the walls

– what's mine, and what's his? At what point did we stop being two separate entities hurtling through life, side by side, and come together into an amalgamation of whatever this mess is that we have become?

I don't consider why my hand pulls the one book from the shelf, a gift from some Christmas some year in a past that's blended itself together into snippets. He'd it made for me, my own name on the front, each page framing one of my own photographs. The smooth cover gives only slightly as I shift it from hand to hand. Each letter of my name is hardly raised, but the edges of my fingertips can still trace each outline, spelling the name I took when I said my vows so many years ago.

He did this for me, some grand gesture of belief or pride, perhaps, or some attempt to push me towards some vision that he still held of who I should be, a vision I could never make into reality. He's been living trapped in denial for so long about who I am, thinking I'm some talented artist or adventurous spirit.

Was that why he turned to someone else, someone who maybe checked all of the boxes in that questionnaire he carried around in his mind?

I tuck the book into my over-sized purse. Other than that and my suitcase, no longer empty, I leave everything else for some other sometime. I pause less than a moment when locking the door. We were so proud when we first bought this house, posing for pictures in front of the "sold" sign. The first time we unlocked this house, our home, we carried champagne in with us, toasting one another and our future in the same living room I just left. Now, my hand hesitates for a single heartbeat as I turn the key.

In almost as little time, I'm sitting behind the wheel of my car, staring straight ahead. I don't remember the walk to the car, don't remember creaking open the back door and heaving in my suitcase. I haven't put the car into drive yet, haven't even turned the ignition. Yet my hands are gripping the wheel, my suitcase on the seat behind me.

This is it. I'm really leaving him.

The question, *"Should I stay?"* begins its inevitable sprint through my mind, opening doors and peering around corners. When it finds its answer, lurking behind a curtain hiding a window smeared with fingerprints, I allow my memory to stare at the tableau unfolded there. Through that window, there stands a much younger version of myself, looking up at a much younger version of the man who became my husband, in a crowded bar one New Year's Eve. Mark is looking at another man, only a boy really, and even from the distance of years and experience, I see the anger etched in the air between them. His eyes are frozen on the boy, his mouth set in a grim line. But nineteen-year-old me wasn't looking at the other boy. I was staring, a little open-mouthed, at this hero who had stepped from every teenage fantasy into my world.

I loved that man, that hero, then. I love him still. But more than that, I love the man he is now. I love the lines that have appeared, stretching from the corners of his eyes. I love the hands that have grown rougher, older, though they haven't reached for me for so long. I love the hair that I woke to this morning, that's receded a bit, but still is dark, still curls in the back. I love the way he drinks his coffee in the mornings, blowing exactly three puffs of breath across the rim of his cup before taking that first sip. Three breaths, every morning. I even love the way he used to mutter to himself while going through those ridiculous piles of marking. I love the way he'd come home, barge through the door, ready to tell me all about this student who did that, or that parent who called about this, or such and such incident featuring so-and-so.

Was that enough to make me stay? Was that fairy tale emotion, concealed within everyday moments, enough for me to forgive him? Enough for me to forgive myself, for staying this long already? For still loving him? For still wanting to stay?

Enough to make me forget holding that phone in my hand?

It was a one-word answer, lurking behind that curtain

hiding that first meeting, that propelled my hand to the key in the ignition. *Should I stay?*

    Why?

CHAPTER 17

Mark, age 43
2016

I close up the books on my desk, piling them according to class and chronology. The bell only rang minutes ago, and already I am rushing.

"When is this due, Mr. Holden?" Mila Ayers hoists her purse higher on her shoulder as she steps around the door. Gone are the days when the students would hover in my room, debating banned books or some bigger theme or conflict in something we studied in class. Now I usher them out, only answering the quickest of questions.

"Tuesday next," I tell Mila, not glancing up as I shove papers into the bag I will lug home, but likely will not even look at tonight. Gone, too, is the extra help I used to offer most days after school.

It turns out that, between my students and my marriage, I chose my marriage.

Not that Danielle asked me to choose. She would never do that, not in so many words. But one of the points stated again and again in Dr. Frost's office was the time issue. How much time, in all honesty, did I need to spend away from home? Work was not the real issue, I knew, but still I watched the clock so much more closely.

Time, Danielle had said. That was what it was going to take to get back to where we were before… well, before everything.

Mila is gone now, a hollered, "Thanks!" over her shoulder as she left. Grabbing my jacket from the back of my chair, I hoist up my marking bag, close the last book - full of grades and percentages - and make my way to the door. The exit to the staff parking lot is down the hall, and I pull my phone out of my pocket so I have something to stare at, just as I do every day. I take particular care to study the screen as I walk past the gymnasium.

I suppose my focus on looking preoccupied is to blame for not actually watching where I'm going. So, the one person I'm trying to avoid is the exact person I physically run into. Of course.

It isn't like a book or movie; her papers don't go flying, I don't stoop to pick them up, we don't share an awkward stare as we both reach for the same paper. Our hands don't brush.

"Sorry," I mumble. But I look up, and have to swallow hard at the expression on her face. Her mouth, those same lips I once tasted, is thin and downturned. Her eyebrows, slightly lifted, framing her eyes, those same ones I stared into with such intimacy, now only offering me a distracted glance. I'm expecting sadness, maybe, or even anger. I am expecting to see some emotion in the coals of the fire that's always been there. But there is only indifference.

"Oh. Hey Mark."

I'd braced myself for something, some scene, some melodrama.

But I did not know how to react to nothing.

"Um… hey." *Oh great. Sort of suave, right?*

"Heading home?"

"Um…. yeah." Another great comeback. *This is not going well.*

111

"Lots of marking?" She lifts her chin in the direction of the bag hanging off my shoulder.

"Yeah." I've moved from stammering "um" like one of my students having to give a presentation, to coherent, monosyllabic responses. Progress.

"Cool. Okay. Guess I'll see you around." She gives a half nod, the same as you would any casual acquaintance.

I step aside as she brushes past me. Is that all I've been reduced to now? A casual acquaintance?

I suppose I should be thankful. There could have been that scene I expected. There could have been yelling and crying and reports of unprofessional conduct. There could have been rumours, which could have gotten back to Danielle, who still has her hand on the door, ready to go. I doubt the suitcase at the top of her closet is empty. It sits there, ready and waiting for my next monumental mistake. If there'd been some kind of altercation that had gotten back to Danielle, I don't think it would have taken much for her to take that suitcase down and pull it right after her, right back out the door.

But that doesn't mean I'm okay with the way Allison just brushed past me. Was it all truly nothing, then? Was every touch, every kiss, every year - yes, it had been *years* of secret liaisons - was it all meaningless? She gave no reaction to her arm touching mine, not so much as a pause or whispered word.

She hadn't cried when I left her that last time. I'd told her before, of course, told her we were done after I found that box in the closet. But then Danielle had left, and I'd called Allison to meet up, to tell her one more time, in person.

There was never a question, though, of me not trying to win back Danielle. I think Allison hated me for that. She wanted me to at least consider a future with her, but I couldn't.

"Maybe," I had told her, "Maybe one day, but I need to at least try to get Danielle to come back first."

"She left you. She packed her bags. She didn't even leave a note. Do you need a parade blaring it out for you to get the message? It's done."

"Not yet. There's a chance, I know there is. And if there is a chance, I have to try."

"So what am I supposed to do? Wait until there are no chances left?"

I reached over and took her hand. She let me, but she didn't let her fingers close around my own.

"I don't know."

She kept her eyes on mine. I was struck, not for the first or hundredth time, of the difference between these two women in my life. Danielle would have been crying, pleading, promising. Allison was even, collected. I wonder now if maybe it was coldness, not confidence, that drove her, but I dismiss the thought as soon as it flitted through my mind. Why spend time focused on her? What good could that possibly serve?

"That isn't good enough for me, Mark," she finally said. She still hadn't taken her hand from mine, still hadn't shifted her eyes away.

"I know. It's just…" I broke the gaze first, trailing off as I regarded the artwork on the wall. It was a landscape, similar to any other in any generic motel room, but I became fascinated by it in an effort to avoid her eyes.

Finally, still staring at the red brushstrokes, I continued, attempting to keep my tone as even and controlled as hers. "I don't think I can do this to her anymore. I told you that."

"Yeah, you told me. But then she left you. I think that changes things a bit, don't you?"

"Not really."

Her head tilted, as if she were one of my students considering a question. "So you lied to me before, all those things you said?"

I shook my head. "I never lied to you. But she's my wife."

"She was."

"She is. She still is."

Allison waved her hand in the air, brushing away the argument. How many times had those same hands been pressed against my chest? How many times had those nails gripped my shoulders? "For now. Technically."

My voice dropped, and I lost any remaining illusion of confidence. "I'm going to get her back, Allison. You need to know that."

"So all those times when she was waiting at home for you, you were with me. And now that she isn't there waiting anymore, now all of a sudden you are so damned concerned, riding some guilt trip about crawling between my legs?"

"Don't be vulgar, Allison."

"Don't be a liar and a cheat, Mark."

I couldn't argue with that, so I said nothing. She still hadn't taken her hand from mine, and I looked at it then, directly at the freckle below her left knuckle that was so faint you could hardly see it if you weren't staring. I didn't even try to stop my finger from tracing that freckle, as if I could etch it into my memory, and with it, every moment between us. Even this one.

She shifted then, turning to resume the staring contest between us. Nothing much was said for a long time, and when she pulled me to her, her whispered promise of "One more for the road" was the only inkling that this time was different from all those other times before.

Of course, I hated myself even more after, but I knew that would be the last time I would reach for Allison, the last time I would allow her to reach for me. I always hear about closure in situations like this, and I always thought it was bullshit, but honestly, maybe there is something to it after all.

Allison had meant something to me. She'd meant a lot to me. If I'm honest, which I'm trying to be again, she still does. But I once made a promise to Danielle. We promised, we kissed, people took pictures, and Danielle grinned so much that she joked her face would stay that way. I broke that promise, just as I've broken all those unspoken, everyday promises made throughout the years. Every time I acted like I was a good husband, hell, even a decent human being, I was breaking a promise.

No more.

So when I crawled out of bed that last time, Allison didn't even try to stop me. Her gaze just followed me as I found my clothes, pulling on each item with a deliberate slowness that dripped with determination in every movement. Each button on my shirt was fastened with purpose, closing my shirt and my resolve to never again remove my clothes with anyone other than the woman I have hurt so many times.

I did not look back until I was dressed, one hand on the door.

"I mean it, you know." It was the first thing I'd said for a long time. There had not been any talking after she reached for me, nothing but sighs and moans and gasps. My voice sounded strange now, as though I'd talked too loudly in a library. I was waiting to be shushed.

"I know." I hadn't specified what I meant, and she didn't ask. It didn't matter. I meant it – all of it. I meant every word spoken tonight, and everything that came after, and everything that came before.

There was still no expression on her face. Maybe she'd been expecting this all along. Maybe she'd never cared.

Still, I hesitated. I knew that when I went through that door, this would all be over.

"Will you be okay?"

Her left eyebrow raised. The shadow of the corner of her lip lifted, for less than a second, then rearranged itself back into its neutral place. "I think I'll manage."

"It's just…" I trailed off again. I didn't know what to say. What else was there to say? I pulled my shoulder blades together, and turned again toward the door, taking a deep breath, ready to face a world without Allison.

"Mark, wait a sec."

I looked back again, quicker than I'd have liked. She had left the bed, pulling the sheet around her so it trailed behind, reminding me of a train at a wedding, and mocking me for the remembrance.

She stepped towards me just as I realized how uncharacteristic the sheet was. Allison was many things, but shy was not one of them. She generally walked around in whatever she was, or was not, wearing. A week ago, she would have jumped from the bed and bounced across the room, leaving the sheet lying in a tangled mess on the bed.

She stopped in front of me.

"What is it?" My voice was quieter, and I fought against the heat spreading through me in response to her nearness.

One pale arm snaked around my neck, and she lifted herself up onto her tiptoes, pressing her lips against the corner of my mouth, holding them there for one of those moments that stretches on through heartbeats and breaths and blinking eyes. When she pulled away, she was softer somehow.

I swallowed. "Allison…"

"Don't." She shook her head, and there was that hint of a smile again. "It's fine, Mark. I just want you to know, well, that it's okay. I'm going to miss you. We had some fun, you know? And I… well, the thing is…" Her usual confidence faltered, and that shook me. She seemed to wrestle with something, and a wave of premonition told me I needed to leave. Right then. Right that very second.

I didn't.

"The thing is," she repeated, "I'm going to say what I need to say, and you can't interrupt or anything, okay? I'm just going to say it, and then you're going to leave without answering, and everything will be fine. Okay?"

I nodded, but otherwise didn't respond. I think now that maybe I should have. It was my last chance, but I didn't take it. Still, what could I have said? I was still leaving.

"Okay. So here it is. Like I said, we had some good times. You were sometimes my favourite part of the day. A lot of times, actually. I just want you to know that I care about you. I did, I mean. But I get it. I always knew what this was. And that was good for me. I sure as hell didn't plan on actually getting attached. But I did, and that's my own fault.

"But I get it. So here's what's going to happen. As soon as you leave this room, that's it. We're just two people who happen to work with some of the same kids. We can go over scheduling and permission forms, but that's it. There's nothing more. I want you and your wife to be super happy and all that. I really do. This whole thing was fun, and good, Mark, but it was probably bad, too. So I'm totally okay. I don't want to talk about this anymore or even think about it anymore.

"Now I need you to leave, Mark. I need you to go, and this time don't stop at the damned door."

I allowed myself one last look at her as I nodded, grabbed my jacket from a nearby chair, and started back through the door.

"Don't turn around this time, Mark."

So I didn't. I didn't even slow down when I thought that I heard her say one last thing to my retreating back. "I loved you, you know."

CHAPTER 18

Mark, age 46
2019

An email circulated through all of the staff at all of the schools in the district. According to the memo, the art gallery in town was working with small businesses in the area to showcase local artists and talents. Although submissions were being accepted from all age groups, we were encouraged to send in student work.

That was not what I was thinking of when I first opened the email, though. I was thinking of Danielle, now in her mid-thirties, still working at that same clothing store that she'd started at years ago now, wandering around our small city with her camera on the weekends, spending hours in the dark room I set up for her in the basement.

That had been one of my projects a few years ago, yet another attempt at an apology. She had smiled a soft "thanks" at the time, told me I "didn't need to do that", and gone back upstairs. Less than a week later, I came home to what seemed to be an empty house. I could feel my heart lurch into my throat. *Gone again.*

It was only after a search through each room that I realized her suitcase was still at the top of her closet, her coffee cup from the morning still by the sink, her purse on the floor by the back door. And that's when I tiptoed downstairs. I knew better than to open the door of the darkroom I'd made her, but I could hear her through the door, and she was humming to herself. Humming.

Danielle is the only person I know who would even use a darkroom. Most people wouldn't even know what one looked like anymore. It had taken hours of research to figure out how to put one together, and I had to order in a lot of the materials from specialty centers in larger cities in the States. When I heard the muffled chorus from "Singing in the Rain" hummed over and over again through that door, I knew that despite all her protestations and shrugs, that those pictures and that camera mattered to her.

So that was why I was more than a little surprised when she refused to submit her photos after I told her about the gallery's call for submissions.

"I'm not interested." She was washing the dishes at the sink while I was packing up leftovers into the individual plastic containers that we each would pack to work the next day.

"Why not?" Portioning out pasta.

"I'm just not."

"But Hun, you've always wanted to -"

"Oh, all of a sudden you are an expert on what I have always wanted?"

"That's not what I meant." I blinked at the back of her head, bent over the suds as she scrubbed at a pot. I knew that tone, and had no desire to get in an argument over this.

"I just said I'm not interested. Leave it at that."

"Okay."

But I didn't. I saw the way she cleaned that camera, the way she ran her fingertips over her favourite framed landscapes, the way she flipped through the albums and scrapbooks that she kept on the top shelf of the bookcase in the living room. I saw all of that, and I was reminded of the young woman - just a girl really - sitting on my couch in that apartment of once-upon-a-time, confessing to wanting to capture the world within the lens of her camera.

I knew that she loved her photographs, and that she was just scared, scared to fail, the way she thought she had way back then. But things were different now. I knew that, too. Oh God, did I know that. I knew that time had changed some things, so that perhaps she was left with only the echo of what she thought was failure, without actually remembering the raw reality of it. She hadn't lost her passion, or her talent. She'd let one speed bump throw her off the road years ago, and now I just wanted her to get behind the wheel again.

I knew it would be like the darkroom. She would profess disinterest, yes, maybe even refusal, but at the end of the day, she would be happy. I would do it for her, if that was what she needed.

And that is how I came to be sitting cross-legged on the floor in the middle of the living room, surrounded by her albums and books, trying to choose the best of her work to submit.

This was the correct course of action. If they accepted her work, she would be thrilled. And if not, she would be none the wiser. But they'd accept her. I knew it.

My untrained eye wasn't sure exactly what to look for. I decided just to pull out the ones that I liked the most, cross my fingers, and wait.

*   *   *

It was weeks later that the envelope came, her name printed on the front, the gallery's logo watermarked in the corner. At first, I had rushed to collect the mail before her after work every day, trying to shield her - and to be honest, myself - from the first shock of whatever news that envelope held. But days had passed, and then weeks, and I'd stopped rushing.

So, when I came home that day, it took me a minute to understand the heaviness in the air. The silence hit me in the face as soon as I opened the door.

There are several types of silences. There are the silences that hold weight to them, one big pause, a breath away from something big and important, even life-changing. There are the silences that are empty, but comfortable. There is no undertone in those silences, just quiet, meandering thought. Then there are the silences that are full of emptiness. If you wander into these silences, you want them to break, you want to shout into them and make them echo, because the "not-saying" is so lonely. Those are the silences of broken promises and heartbreak, when you walk into an empty house and realize that the suitcase that was always in your wife's closet is gone.

That was the silence that hit me when I came home that day.

The envelope was on sitting on the coffee table in the living room, torn open, but not empty. She had shoved the paper back.

I didn't bother to find out what the letter said before pushing towards the kitchen. I rounded the corner, bracing myself to find the room empty, but there she was, her back to me, scouring the top of the stove.

"Hi, Honey." I stepped closer to her, and even to my own ears my voice sounded too high-pitched, too timid.

Her eyes remained focused on the burnt-on stains and faded glass.

"How was work?" I tried again, and this time I sounded a little better.

Her mouth tightened into a thin line, but still, she didn't look up. Still, she scrubbed, back and forth, back and forth, in the same spot.

I waited, considered. Should I leave the room, retreating slowly as though from a wild animal? Should I apologize for sending in her work? She clearly would have figured out that I did it. Should I try to explain? Should I just quietly go about my business, hoping that if I act normally, things will somehow just become normal? Should I try, again, to talk to her?

At least she was still here. At least that suitcase was still at the top of her closet, at least she was still in our kitchen, at least she hadn't thrown that dish at my head when she first heard my footsteps.

"Did you have a good day?" I figured if she didn't answer this time, I would wait and try again later.

She stopped her maniacal scrubbing, and her shoulders raised, fell, and pushed themselves back. The back of her head straightened, and a voice in the back of my head began wishing that she would go back to scrubbing.

"Did I have a good day? Is that what you are asking me?" I could barely hear her measured voice from where I hovered in the doorway.

"Yeah…" I stammered. Anything, everything I said was going to be wrong. "I was just… you know… wondering…."

"Right. You were wondering. Because you are so concerned about me and how I spend my days."

"Hold on a minute." I knew she was upset, and I knew there would be a fight, but I wasn't about to start off this way.

"No." She turned, shaking her head, her hair falling across her eyes as she did so. "No. You hold on a minute." She breathed so deeply I could see her chest rise and fall. "Can you please explain to me why I got a letter from the art gallery today?"

I shifted from one foot to the other. There was no way this was going to go well. What would make her the least upset?

"Oh? Did you get a letter?"

"Yes, I got a letter. From the art gallery. About my photographs and a show I have apparently applied to be in."

"Yeah? That's cool, Honey. What did the letter say?"

"I don't care what the letter says." She tossed the scrub pad down onto the stove, hard enough it bounced up slightly before coming to a stop.

This was worse than I thought. "Look, I know you are probably upset…."

She snorted.

"And you have every right to be…"

Another snort, with a slight head nod and lift of the eyebrows.

"But I need you to know, I only wanted what's best for you."

"Oh, right. Because you are the expert on what's best for me."

"Well, kind of."

Oops. Shit. The words are out, floating around in the air between us, heavy clouds threatening acid rain.

Wrong answer. Danger, danger, backtrack.

"I mean, well, no. Of course not. Not like you are. I don't know more than you, I mean."

"Really? So you don't know as much about me as I do, and yet you went against my wishes and took something of mine and put it out there without my permission. Not only without my permission. After I specifically told you not to!"

I had no trouble hearing her voice now.

"I know, I know."

"Don't use that tone with me, Mark. I am not some child, some student of yours you need to talk to that way. Stop it."

"I'm not meaning to use any tone with you…"

"And you weren't meaning to go through my things - *steal* my things - and send them away, either, right?"

"That isn't what I…"

"I'm sure it isn't. I'm sure you were just so goddamned well-intentioned. Perfect Mark has to make Danielle fit into his perfect world."

She brushed past me as she left the kitchen. I didn't know where she was planning on going. Maybe the living room, so we could stand and yell at each other from equal sides of a bigger space, so one of us wasn't in a doorway. Maybe she just needed to walk, to pace, to stomp, while she yelled out her frustrations. I just knew one thing: I couldn't let her get near her closet, couldn't let her see the empty suitcase sitting at the top, reminding her. I turned to follow her.

"What is that supposed to mean?" Better she be angry and yelling than resigned and packing.

"You know what it means."

"No I don't."

"Did I stutter?" She spun to face me, planting her feet to the hardwood.

"Danielle…."

"Mark…" The mocking was blatant, the sound of a child mimicking a younger sibling.

"That isn't helpful, Danielle."

"I'm sure it isn't." She turned to face me. "But you know what else isn't helpful? Doing exactly what I told you I didn't want to do. You took my pictures, Mark, and sent them in. *My* pictures. Not yours. You knew I didn't want you to do that. Didn't you?"

"Yeah, I did."

"And you did it anyway."

"Yeah."

She looked around the room, raised her arms as though to gesture, but then dropped them at her side, limp. "Then why did you do it?"

How could I explain this to her? "Look, Danny, I know you didn't want to… I know you asked me not to… but you are just so talented. I've always thought so. So talented, and it would just be so great to have other people see that talent."

She blinked, biting her lips. "But you knew I didn't want to… knew I didn't even want to talk about it."

"Hun, I know you're scared…"

"Scared?! Scared. What the hell do you know about it?"

"I know that you're an artist. A photographer. Not just someone who takes a picture or two on the weekend or on holidays. An actual photographer. And for some reason you're content just working in a shop and not…"

"This exactly what I'm talking about." Her voice rose again, sharpened itself to a point in her words. "Perfect Mark in his perfect life can't handle having a wife who only works in a shop."

"That isn't what I meant. That isn't why…"

"Is that why you went to her, Mark? Went to someone who didn't just work in a shop?"

"What the hell are you talking about?"

"Is that why you found someone else to spend your time with? Someone who looks the perfect way and plays the perfect part?"

"Damn it, Danielle!" I can count on one hand the number of times that I've raised my voice in anger at my wife. This was one of them.

She blinked again, but didn't respond.

"I screwed up, okay? I screwed up, and I apologized. I'm not proud of what happened, but it happened. It's done."

"You screwed up? You screwed a lot, didn't you? Don't try to make it sound like it was a one-time thing. You went back to her, again and again…. All those times…"

"Yes, I did. I did. I admitted it, didn't I? I told you what happened. I told you I was sorry. I will keep telling you I'm sorry every day if you want me to. That won't change what happened. But for the love of god, is this going to be what we live with for the rest of our lives? Are we ever going to move past this?"

"Move past this? Are you kidding me?"

"Is that what it's going to be like, Danielle? 'You have to take out the garbage now, because you slept with another woman. You have to do the dishes, because you slept with another woman. You have to buy me this, because you slept with another woman. You have to agree with everything I say, because you slept with another woman. You're wrong in every disagreement, because you slept with another woman.' Is that it? Is that what you're turning into?"

Of course I regretted it the instant the words left my mouth, sailed across the room, and settled themselves into her eyes, into those pools of hurt and confusion and shock. I saw the words there, letters mocking me as they played in the anguish.

I stood, looking at her. She hadn't answered, hadn't spoken at all. All of the anger had poured out of me and settled with those words, and I was left with a hardened stomach and tightened chest.

I swallowed once, twice. "Look, Danielle…" I began, my voice almost softened to normalcy, another apology hidden somewhere along the edges. "I didn't mean…"

But she raised her hand to stop me, and shook her head. She didn't want me to finish my sentence. She just looked at me, her fingers slowly curling in, her hand slowly returning to her side.

She walked straight past me, straight to the door. *Don't go. Don't go. Not again.* I willed her to stay with every ounce of me, but I didn't move, didn't speak, didn't even allow my eyes to glance towards the bedroom, and her closet.

She paused at the door, and spoke to it when she said, each word measured against the previous, "I'm going for a walk."

When she closed the door, a breath I didn't know I had been holding escaped.

*   *   *

They accepted her work. She calmed down. I don't know if she ever really forgave me, but I have so many transgressions tallied against me, I am not sure if this one is even matched against the rest.

As it is, her photographs will be displayed throughout May at the gallery, along with the other nine finalists in this local artist endeavour. Then hers will spend the rest of the summer hanging in one of the coffee shops in town. In fact, they've requested that she send in more, to fully line the walls. They want her to write up titles and descriptions and price tags for the ones that she'd be willing to sell. She can't quite believe that someone would be willing to actually pay for her photographs, but she agreed to come up with something, anyway.

We haven't spoken about the fact that I went against her wishes by submitting her work. I tried to bring it up once, even promised I wouldn't touch her work again, but she just shook her head and changed the subject. If she's willing to let it alone, at least for now, I am not going to stir it up.

I know she is still hurt. I see it sometimes, when she looks at me. I see my own words, still there, settled in her eyes. But even though I know I didn't do the right thing, I am still not entirely convinced it was the wrong thing.

CHAPTER 19

Danielle, age 41
2022

I went shopping with my mother yesterday. She wanted a dress for Aunt Melinda's funeral. I thought any black dress would do, but apparently I was wrong.

Aunt Melinda was one of those crazy people who lived by their own set of ideals. She was actually Mom's cousin, just a few years older than her, am I'm not sure that two more different people could exist in the same family. Mom is straightforward, focused on her reputation, a woman who spends thousands on hair stylists and manicures and all the latest fashions. She got married at the right age, had kids at the right age, two kids, the white picket fence, everything.

Aunt Melinda ran around barefoot everywhere she went during the warmer seasons. She wore draping layers, in every colour, often altered by her own hand. She grew her own vegetables and sold jams at farmers' markets. She taught herself to paint when she was in her fifties, because it was something she'd always wanted to do and never had. She would go years without cutting her hair, and then shave one side off, leaving the other side with a short asymmetrical bob, which she would then dye some extraordinary colour. The last time had been neon green, which was quite a sight with her grey roots.

Melinda had never married. She was one of those poor souls my mother referred to, who would age and die alone, sad and forgotten. Images of a dark, dusty bed, an old woman withering away, surrounded by cats were always invoked when my mother hypothesized about Melinda's end.

She died following a stroke she had during a ski trip.

I've had family members die, but this one seemed to be hitting Mom harder than the others, so I agreed to go shopping with her. I steeled myself for a day of hell, and picked her up.

To be fair, the comments about my car and appearance were fewer than usual, so I began to relax a bit and asked her about Dad. He wasn't taking the death of his cousin-in-law well either, as it meant he'd lost his favourite holiday drinking buddy.

Mom was actually really well-behaved all day. I was leery about this, put even more on guard than usual. She was pleasant, polite. I was waiting for the implosion.0

It didn't come, which is part of the reason I'm so focused on the day even now, a day and some later, lying in bed, watching a fly buzz around the light outside the window.

The rest of the reason is something bigger. Something much, much bigger.

She said she was proud of me.

I'd taken her to the coffee shop where I have a few photos hanging. Ever since Mark submitted my work to the gallery that time, which I try not to think about, I've had pieces exhibited there rather consistently.

I'm not ashamed to say I had ulterior motives for taking my mother to that particular shop. I wanted to show her the photographs. I wanted her to be impressed with me, even a little.

I pointed them out to her while we were waiting for our lattes. She studied them, standing in front of each as though she was in an art gallery in a big city. She even sidestepped around one couple at a table in front of one of the frames, invading their personal space just so she could get a closer look at a waterfall image.

She didn't say much, just that they "were nice." She didn't ask questions or make comments as we collected our drinks and headed back out to the car.

From the passenger side, though, once we hit the highway, she began to talk about Melinda.

"She did a lot, you know," she said at last, after chatting about the details of the upcoming funeral. "She didn't have kids, so she missed out on that. But she did a lot."

I kept my eyes on the road. I could sense the unspoken question in the air, that wondering about children.

But she continued, letting the question dissipate.

"She went to a lot of places. Saw a lot of things. One thing about Melinda, she didn't back down from stuff. She wanted to see the pyramids, she bought a plane ticket. She wanted to learn to paint, she took a class. She wanted to spend all day in her pyjamas, she did just that. I always... I always thought that was pretty great, the way she was like that." She took a sip of her latte. "The way you're kind of like that."

"Me?" I whispered the question, then hated that I did. I knew better than to interrupt, knew better than to break the spell.

But I hadn't. She kept talking.

"Yeah. The pictures, for example. I wouldn't do something like that, put my name out there on something, letting people see it and judge it. Judge me. No thank you.

"But I sometimes wish I could. Do that, like you did. Like Melinda would have. I'd be proud of myself for something like that.

"Like you should be. Like I'm proud of you."

I didn't drive the car into the ditch or oncoming traffic

then, and for that I'm rather impressed. I didn't know what to say, how to react.

So I didn't.

I kept my eyes straight ahead, wrapping my hands around the steering wheel so tightly my fingernails dug indentations into the leather.

My heart was racing, pounding in my ears. If there was honking, I wouldn't have heard.

I drove the rest of the way to her house like that, focused only on the road and my own whirling emotions. Before I knew it, I'd pulled up to the curb outside the condominium building she and Dad had moved into a few years back.

She stepped out of the car, yanked open the back door, and hefted out her bags. Shutting the back one again with a jerk of her hip, she shifted all her bags to one hand so she could smooth her hair down with the other.

I watched her, watched this ritual, and said nothing. I wanted to say something, say everything, but my brain and my voice were having trouble working together. When I opened my mouth, all that came out was a series of incomprehensible mumbles.

"Pardon?" My mother leaned back down, so she could poke her head back into the car.

"Just… just wanted to say thanks, Mom. And I hope the dress is what you wanted. And…?

"And?"

My confidence, what little I had, shattered. "And you looked good in it."

"Thank you, Danielle." She straightened again, smoothed her hair back again. Then she evened out the distribution of her packages between her hands, and nodded at me. "And thank you for driving me."

She closed the door and turned, then took two, three, four steps away from the car.

I rolled down the window.

"Mom!"

She turned.

"Mom, I just wanted to say…."

She waited.

"Just wanted to say, thank you. I mean it, thank you. And, and I'm proud of you too."

As the words sailed from my mouth to her ears I realized that they were true. Things had been bad, at least between her and my dad. I think they'd been bad in many ways in her life. And she hadn't given up. She still showed up for us, even when she didn't have to, even when she didn't want to, even when we didn't want her too.

She nodded, then resumed her trek to the building. Before she turned, though, I thought I saw a ghost of a smile threaten to crack through.

CHAPTER 20

Mark, age 50
2023

I remember that once upon a time people actually used to call one another on their phones. I know how old I sound when I say that, but it's true. So I also knew that when the phone rang last Tuesday, it would be someone quite a bit older than me. I was right. My father wanted to meet for "lunch or coffee or something" to attempt to "catch up".

My first thought was that someone had died. But after I was assured that Mom was still okay, I agreed to meet him for lunch.

So now I'm sitting here, at this table, chugging water, waiting and wondering. When I was a child, whenever I'd done something wrong, he'd tell me to go to my room and wait for him to show up to talk to me, which resulted in me hiding under my covers or sulking at my desk, imagining the very worst of every possible and impossible scenario. That was, of course, the whole point.

But that was years ago, decades even. I'm a grown man now. Hell, I'm middle-age. My elderly father is hardly going to be able to lecture me, hardly going to be able to strike fear and shame through me.

And yet, I'm still anxious.

So as he walks in, I have to dry my palms on the legs of my jeans. He nods, says my name in greeting, and sits across from me.

I wait.

Nothing.

I empty the rest of my glass, set it down, and look through the side of the empty glass, watching remaining droplets slide down. My father is skewed from this angle. The world is skewed from this angle.

Probably not the best idea to be squinting through a water glass like a child. I straighten. He's holding one of the menus that the waiter left, but he's watching me, saying nothing.

"Well, how's it going, Dad?" Perhaps he's waiting for an invitation.

"Fine."

"How's Mom?"

"Fine, too. She sends her love."

"Thanks. Take back mine?"

"Of course."

Okay, now what? I watch the way my father's hands tap at the edge of the menu. I remember those hands, pointing out words to me as I read along in picture books, him stretched out on the couch beside me. When did those hands get so wrinkled? When did those spots start showing up? I glance down at my own hands. They don't look like they used to either. Nothing looks like they used to.

"How's Danielle?" My father closes the menu and sets it aside, evening his gaze at me.

"She's good. Works a lot. Stays busy."

He looks up at the chandelier hanging above our table. It's some sort of attempt at modernism. Or maybe postmodernism. Who the hell even knows anymore?

"Got something to say, Dad?"

"Just wondering how she is, is all," he says to the light.

"Uh huh."

His eyes drop back to mine. "Let's order."

I nod. *Fine by me.* The awkwardness between us has settled in the center of our table like a bird nesting down. A vulture maybe. I am more than willing to make the damned thing wait.

Neither of us say much while we wait for the waiter to come to our table. We comment on the restaurant, on the menu, on our orders. I ask about his drive, and he mentions the weather. Finally, though, the food is ordered, the glasses filled, and the silence stretches out in front of us.

"You may as well just say it," I begin.

"What?"

"Whatever you came here to say."

"Can't a father just want to have lunch with his son?"

I snort. "Not unless we are on a rerun of some after-school special or something."

He smiled. "One thing about you, Mark, you don't take the bullshit." He sighs, looking around the restaurant. "Thing is, there really isn't a reason. I just wanted to see you."

"You did?" I think of the way he shuffled to the table when he first came in. Is his age catching up to him?

"Yeah, I did, Son." *Son.* When he starts calling me "Son", it's not a good sign.

"You okay, Dad?"

He smiles at me, and I'm struck, not for the first or last time, by the wrinkles around his eyes, creased into his face.

My own lines have started appearing in identical places.

One day, I could be a mirror image of this old man sitting in front of me. Only not quite mirrored; there will be no "Son" for me to talk to when I'm sitting on that side of the table.

"Yeah. I'm good. It's just, you get to a certain stage in life, and you start to wonder. I mean, hell, happens to every man, I think. Women too, probably. You'd have to ask your mother about that one."

"Wonder? What are you getting at, Dad?"

His shoulders, once wide enough for me to sit on as he strolled down the street, now rise and fall.

"I don't even know. Just wonder. About life I guess." He snorts, a hollow, dismissive sound. "Forget it. Forget I said anything. My mind wanders sometimes."

"It does? How long has that been going on?"

"Probably since you started giving me grey hair the day you turned twelve."

I smile. I know this story, have heard it four times a year since I actually was twelve, but still I play along.

"I did not give you grey hair when I was twelve."

"Sure you did. You and that other kid, that one you were always chumming around with... What was his name?"

"Charlie."

"That's right, Charlie Hamilton."

My muscles relax. Regardless of the fact that this is a familiar story, if he can remember the surname of my childhood friend, maybe his mind wasn't wandering so much after all.

"Yeah, Dad. Charlie Hamilton."

"Yeah. And the two of you walked in the door, pleased as can be, and you were all banged up, and your arm was broken, and I'm not understanding why you aren't screaming your head off at the pain. And then Charlie. Charlie Hamilton starts talking about some jump you hit with your bike. Says you went tearing down a huge hill and off the jump. Flew through the air. I tell you you're lucky to have only broken your arm and you're going to end up with scars. And you, little twelve-year-old you, you turn to me and say, 'Aw, that's okay, Dad. Girls like boys with scars if they can fly.'"

I shake my head when I'm supposed to, and laugh when I'm supposed to.

"You always did like the girls, Mark."

"Guess so." I'm still chuckling. I want to change the subject, though, so I do. Besides, I'm concerned. "Tell me more about your mind wandering."

"Ah, I'm just getting old. What about you?"

"My mind doesn't wander."

"If you say so." He sits up straighter, stretching his arms to the side. On one, weathered and wrinkles and faded, is an old tattoo. I asked about it once, and he always refused to answer where it came from and what it meant.

"So how's work?"

Work was, well, work. It was awkward still, with me still taking longer routes through the hallways to avoid the gym during volleyball season. I heard she was living with someone now. Well, good for her. It seems that should have made things easier, but it didn't. The students were great, as per usual, but that was part of it, too: *as per usual.* The drama in the staffrooms and staff meetings, the policies and paperwork was getting to be a bit too much. The lessons and lectures and projects and mountains and mountains of marking and planning, too, was getting to be a bit, to be honest, monotonous.

"It's fine." I flag down the waiter and order a drink. I need something stronger than water. I need some scotch in this glass.

"Drinking at lunch?" My father raises his eyebrow as soon as the waiter turns away.

"What about it, Dad? I'm a grown-up. I'm allowed to have a drink at lunch."

"Of course you are. I was just making an observation."

I sigh.

"You sure you're fine, Mark?"

I release the muscles in my hand, surprised to realize I was clutching the napkin. I stretch out my fingers, and stare at the bumps and lines on each, at the simple band circling that fourth finger.

"Yeah. I'm fine."

The noises of the restaurant stretch between us. I catch myself tapping the edge of the table, as my father had been doing to the menu. I wrap my hand around my glass of scotch, just delivered to the table.

I turn my attention to the rest of the restaurant. A pretty waitress dips her chin at me, and I return her smile.

When I shift back to my father, he is looking at me, his lips pressed into a thin line, all amusement wiped from his expression.

"What now?"

His eyebrows furrow, but he says nothing.

"Drop it, Dad. Whatever it is. Drop it."

"Didn't say a word."

"I know what you're thinking."

"Do you? Enlighten your father."

"I'm not allowed to be polite to someone in a restaurant?"

I watch his hand clench around the spoon. Just as he opens his mouth in what I can only assume is a seething retort, he's saved, or perhaps I'm saved. The server - not the pretty waitress, though – arrives at our table with our orders.

When we're alone again, he's unclenched his spoon, and instead has gone back to tapping, this time a light and quick rhythm on the table, a blurry vibration of annoyance.

"Well?" I start again, leaning back in the chair, ignoring the steak sandwich in front of me.

"I'm old, Mark, but I'm not blind. I'm not stupid." He takes a sip of his water, then brings a spoonful of soup to his mouth, watching me the whole time.

I arch an eyebrow. "Meaning?"

He looks down then, taking another swallow of soup before answering with a single word. "Mark."

My name isn't said as a question, just stated, as simple and harsh as the truth.

My silence is my answer, and he knows it.

Another slurp of soup. A bit sloshes over the edge of his spoon, a victim of a hand shaking so minutely.

When did his hands start their vibrations? When did his mind start to wander? When did my father become old? And doesn't that mean that I, too, am becoming old?

"I just was being polite to a waitress," I say to his bent head.

"I know."

Another cut, another bite. I have nothing to say, so it's better my mouth is full. He came with an agenda, and I'm determined to let him get it all out.

"You never know what can happen. Time's a funny thing."

"Mmmhmmm," I mumble around a mouthful of steak and bread.

"Time goes by, quicker than you can imagine." He gulps at another spoonful. He dabs his mouth with his napkin, missing some broth on his whiskers. He picks up his spoon again, and jabs it into the air, punctuating his points. "Travel. Write. Read. Renovate the house. Watch TV in the middle of the day. Take a class together. Take up gardening. I don't know." He dips his spoon into the soup one more time, and scrapes it against the bottom of the bowl. "I wish I was young enough to do it all still myself."

"I'm not that young."

"No." He looks up, his eyes wide, his smile soft. "No, I don't suppose you are." He tears off a chunk of break and swipes it around his bowl, soaking up any remnants. "But you're not yet old, either."

My jaw aches, and I realize I've been clenching my teeth. I put down my knife and fork and use my fingertips to massage my cheek.

My father watches me, pausing in his soup clean-up.

"You're a good man, you know."

Hot and cold alternates flowing through me. "Am I?"

"Of course you are. Don't worry." He looks at the bowl again, giving it one more swipe before lifting the bread to his mouth and biting off a piece. He turns his gaze back to me and tilts his head as he chews.

He swallows the bread. I can see his adam's apple shift up and down, the skin on his neck loose, with a mole that I don't recognize. Crumbs of his crust of bread meet with the broth left in his whiskers.

"Don't worry," he says again. "You'll figure it out."

CHAPTER 21

Danielle, age 46
2027

Jaimie is staying here for a couple of weeks. When Calvin called and explained about their trip through Europe, he didn't even need to ask. I volunteered before he even listed the countries they would be visiting. Of course their daughter could stay with us.

She's almost ten now, a wonderful and terrible age, where she is playing with my makeup and also dolls. She rolls her eyes a lot, but still wears pyjamas with little colourful cartoon dinosaurs all over them.

We cooked together last night. I showed her how to make lasagna. She didn't cook much at home, so I got to show her how to brown beef, chop veggies, layer everything up just right.

Mark has always talked about how rewarding it is to have a student figure something out. That was before, of course, when he was still working full-time. At the beginning of this school year, he switched to half-time, and stopped talking to me so much about work. I'd ask how his day was, or his afternoon, and he'd say, "Fine" and head to work on whatever project had his attention that day.

So I stopped asking.

But I caught a glimpse of what he was talking about last night, as Jaimie danced around the kitchen, chattering about her friends and her parents and a movie she watched, a wooden spoon in her hand, stirring the meat sauce.

I even showed her my secret ingredients; it's not like I have someone else to pass it down to, after all.

She had pink fuzzy socks, and was slipping everywhere. She sped to the fridge and slid past it, crashing into the counter instead. She found the cheese, then sped back and slid to the other counter, all the while singing and wiggling to some awful song.

"Auntie Danny, what do we do now?" she asked again and again. "And then?" Sliding across the floor. "And then?" Bobbing her head as she grates cheese. "How about now?" Layering noodles.

We were washing dishes when Mark came through.

"Smells good, girls."

"Uncle Mark! We're making lasagna. You have totally got to try it. And Auntie Danny showed me her secret recipe, but I had to promise to never tell anyone ever."

"Oh yeah? And what's the secret, Jaimie?"

She rolled her eyes again. "Very funny. I'm not falling for that one. So lame."

He chuckled and wiggled his eyebrows at me. I shrugged in response, my hands soapy wet from the frying pan I was scrubbing.

"And we have enough for leftovers." Jaimie was still talking as she dried the coffee cup in her hand. "Auntie Danny said we could use the fancy plates since I made dinner. But they can't go in the dishwasher and that's why we're doing all these dishes. I never have to do dishes at home since the dishwasher takes everything. But I don't mind. It's part* of being the chef

I think. Don't you?"

Mark chuckled again.

"What's so funny?"

"Nothing. And yes, I think it's part of being the chef."

"And the dishes?"

"What about them?"

"Can we use the fancy dishes? Auntie Danny says you got them for your wedding. And that must have been forever ago."

"Yeah." His smile faltered. "Something like forever ago." He lifted his eyes, meeting mine for a fraction of time before dropping them again. "If it's okay with Auntie Danny, you can certainly use the fancy dishes." The corners of his lips twitched. "Call me when dinner's ready. I'm heading down to the basement."

I didn't ask what he was working on down there. To be honest, I wasn't sure I cared.

I'm not sure that Jaimie has stopped talking since she got here, except of course when she's sleeping. Then the night seems even quieter, the silence stretching around the television set and the book and everything else that Mark and I use to fill our time and focus.

Today, though, I'm doing laundry while Jaimie is out in the yard with Mark. I empty the dryer into the basket and hoist it up onto my hip, shifting sideways to slip through the doorway without dropping the basket full of colourful socks and graphic t-shirts. When I readjust, I look out the window.

They're out there, both kneeling in the dirt. She's wearing an extra pair of his gloves, which are so oversized on her it's a little comical. It's probably good she is resting her hands on her knees; surely they would fall off otherwise. Her hair is up in a ponytail, her head tilted slightly as she watches him, talking and gesturing and pointing to this plant and that plant.

I don't know whether I wince at the nausea that sweeps through me, or the tightness at the back of my throat, but my vision blurs. The scene plays out in slow motion, each nod of her head, each wave of his hand. He says something. She laughs. She reaches out and pulls a weed. She holds it out to him. He pats her on the back.

I gasp, and turn away. I can't watch anymore. My heart hurts too much.

Stumbling from the window, I move into the bedrooms. Better to work on this laundry, better to tidy and clean and focus on something else.

I set the basket down on the bed, heaving my shoulders, struggling to gain control of my emotions.

Deep breaths. In and out.

It's been awhile since I've been so caught off-guard. It used to be that the smallest thing would set me off. Once I was walking downtown and a woman passed me pushing a stroller. That was it - a scene which I witnessed so many times. But that one day, it was too much, and I had to duck into a public bathroom to cry in private.

That was years ago, though, long enough that I'd forgotten to be on guard, forgotten to fortify that wall, so now just one image let it crumble.

Deep breaths. In and out.

My hands are shaking as I reach out to start taking items out of the basket. I stare at my hand, willing the tremors to stop.

They don't, so I give up, and sit beside the basket instead, looking around this room, most often used for storage, but right now home to kicked-off runners, an assortment of hair accessories, and a colourful suitcase covered with flowers. I grip the white edge of the basket hard enough to keep my hand from shaking, hard enough for the hard plastic to bite into my hand.

Deep breaths. In and out.

They looked so perfect out there together. That was the way things were supposed to be. There were supposed to be toys, and lessons, and arguments, and dancing around the kitchen, and afternoons doing chores, and mountains of laundry.

Things don't always turn out the way they're supposed to, though.

I take a shaky breath and clear my throat. A sniff and a toss of my head help clear my mind and my eyes.

Deep breaths. In and out.

I square my shoulders and stand up, lean over the basket, and pick up one of Jaimie's shirts, folding it and setting it aside.

I can do this. Just keep folding, just keep living, just keep breathing.

CHAPTER 22

Danielle, age 54
2035

Mark spent this afternoon golfing, which wasn't odd. I know it keeps him busy and active, so I can't complain about it. And it's not like I don't appreciate the alone time.

But there is something odd now as I hear the door close, announcing his return. I'm in the living room reading. Even after all the developments in technology and entertainment, I still prefer a good old-fashioned book.

"Danielle?" he called me from the entryway.

"Yeah?" I look up, using my thumb as a temporary bookmark while I wait for a response.

"Can you come here please?"

The roll of my eyes isn't intentional, but I don't stop it either. I find my actual bookmark - a beaded leather piece from my store - and set my book aside.

I stretch as I stand. I get stiff quicker than I used to. Once upon a time I could read all day, shifting positions, even hanging upside down off the couch. Now my knees and back creak a little, and I rub a tight spot in my lower back as I head for the entry.

"What is it?" I ask as I get closer. When I see him, though, I stop short. He's standing there, in the khaki pants and polo shirt he wore golfing, holding a bouquet of pink roses.

I raise an eyebrow but say nothing.

"When was the last time I brought you flowers?"

"I don't remember," I lie. It was 2015, a week after he told me about the affair. It was a mixed bouquet then, big on the daisies. He hadn't made a big show about it, just brought it in and left it on the counter while he grabbed a vase from the cupboard above the fridge. He didn't say anything as he filled the vase, put the flowers in it, and set it in the middle of the table.

It was so hard for me to look at him in those days, hard for me to even hear his voice or smell his aftershave in the bathroom in the morning.

But I looked at him then, and he met my gaze and shrugged. "I know flowers can't make up for anything or even come close to an apology, but I thought maybe they could help brighten your day." He shrugged again then. I remember noticing the red lining his eyes, his chapped lips, the spot on his jaw he missed shaving.

"What are the roses for?" I ask, bringing myself back to the present, back to the entryway and the middle-aged man in front of me, and away from the kitchen and the adulterer I still struggled some days to forgive.

"I know roses are cheesy, but I thought pink wasn't as bad as red." He thrust his hand out to me, and I take the flowers. A quick glance confirms it: a full dozen.

"They're lovely. Thank you." He's still standing there, looking at me looking at him.

I watch the rise and fall of his chest as he takes a deep breath and shrugs. I blink away the memory of that other version of this man, that other shrug.

"I was thinking," he says, "that our anniversary is coming up."

"Yeah."

"I know we don't have any plans for it yet this year."

"This year? When was the last time we did anything specific for our anniversary?" I'm not angry or disappointed, just confused. What is he talking about? Where is he going with this?

"Yeah I guess. Just, I thought I would take you out this year."

"Out?"

"Yeah, to dinner."

"For our anniversary?"

"Yes, but I sort of thought we should go tonight instead."

"Tonight?" I realize I'm repeating everything he says as a question, and I don't particularly care. A younger, thinner version of me used to worry how she sounded in front of everyone. Even Mark. Especially Mark.

I haven't seen that girl in a while.

"Yeah. I was able to get reservations for seven, for somewhere that's supposed to be pretty good. If you want to go."

"We're going somewhere that needs reservations?"

"That's the plan. Reservations and a jacket and tie."

"We're dressing up?"

"If you want to go, yeah." He finally kicked his shoes off, pushing on each heel with the toes from the other foot.

He padded past me into the kitchen. "Probably want to put those in some water."

I followed him, but laid the bouquet on the counter, crossing my arms and evening my gaze on him.

"Not that I'm not interested in going, but is there a particular reason you want to take me out tonight?"

"Our anniversary…"

"Is not for a week yet. Try again."

He nods, and looks out the window. "You're right," he admits.

"And?"

He shifts his weight from side to side. *Shit, it must be bad.*

Finally, he turns back to me. He's chewing on his bottom lip, like he always does when he's nervous.

"What is it Mark?"

"Allison."

That word - her name - reaches out and punches me in the gut. I'm sure my heart has stopped. I grow cold, and know that the colour has drained from my face. I grab the counter behind me with a trembling hand, because there is a pretty good chance I'm about to pass out.

The counter won't do much good, though, because my hands are so slick with sweat that if my knees give I will slide straight to the floor regardless of what I'm trying to hold onto.

I don't say anything, but I'm sure I wouldn't be heard over the sound of my gulping breaths anyway.

He's shifting his attention to the window, the floor, the ceiling, darting quick looks at me.

At last he clears his throat. "I saw her today."

My vision swims. *I can do this.* Taking another deep breath, then another, then another, I summon the strength to speak. "You said you would never see her again."

"I didn't mean to."

"You said you'd never say her name in this house."

"I know."

"So...?"

He sighs. "I'm trying to be honest with you. I ran into her is all. Didn't mean to see her. Didn't go looking for her or anything. I haven't seen her since she left the school, and that was before I did."

"So you've said."

"It's the truth."

"Mmhmm." I close my eyes, focusing on pushing down the bile threatening to rise. "So you saw her?" My eyes stay closed.

"Yeah. I saw her. Just quickly. Said hi. She's living with someone you know. Has been for years, I guess."

"I don't care, Mark." His name bites at the space between

us.

"I know."

I open my eyes at last and watch him rubbing the back of his neck, staring at the flowers on the counter.

"What happened?" I'm whispering, afraid of the answer.

"Nothing happened. We chatted for a minute. Maybe less."

"Then why flowers? Why dinner reservations?"

He had to be making up for something, trying to assuage a guilty conscience.

His lips press together and curl up at one corner. There is a gloss to his eyes, still turned toward the flowers. "That's the thing. Nothing happened. But, I was standing there talking to her, and I just started thinking…" He pauses, rubbing the back of his neck again. "I don't know how to explain."

"Try." I finally stop shaking and cross my arms in front of my chest in an attempt to hold myself together, an attempt to appear stern and not terrified.

He nods and sighs again, dropping his hand.

"A lot of time has gone by. And looking at her, listening to her talk, I guess I sort of remembered it all. I remembered being with her…"

"I can't listen to this."

"No, just wait." His hand waves through the air in front of him in an attempt to wipe away his words. "I just mean what it was to spend time with her, to be with her. And I realized something…" I can hear a deep breath that he hisses out through his teeth.

"It wasn't worth it." He's staring at the ground.

"What?"

"It wasn't worth it. All the sneaking around and lying. It's been years, and there is this scar between us. A huge wound. And it's my fault, and I know it will never be able to be totally healed."

What can I say? What is there to say? I'm aware of the neon green light on the stove, the time glaring out from me. There are dishes in the sink, a ring from a teacup on the counter. He used to be the only one who drank tea, and I used to think it was so sophisticated, so scholarly and grown up. Sometime over the years I stopped cleaning up every crumb, I stopped washing and putting away every dish as soon as I had used it. And I started drinking tea, weaker than he ever did.

I ignore the dishes, the tea ring, the time on the clock. I ignore the words hanging in the air between us, stronger than the scent of the roses I lift and arrange in the vase from the top of the fridge.

He's watching me, I know. I can feel it, but I also know his movements and his thoughts and his reactions. I know, without looking, that he hasn't moved, that he hasn't shifted one iota save the direction of his eyes.

I set the vase in the center of the table, adjusting a stem here and there. My fingertips trace over the petals, brushing aside droplets of water from the sink and my attempts to find a way to respond to him.

"I'm trying to think of what to say," I tell him, my attention still on the flowers. "Something profound. Something about roses and thorns. Or that wound and scar thing you said, that was good." I drop my hand, and turn to him. Yes, he was still watching me. "But I don't have the words, Mark. I used up all my words about this years ago. I did all my screaming and yelling and crying and heartaches then. I tried to find the words, the reasons. Tried to figure out why the hell you would do that to me. To us."

His head bobs once, twice.

"But you know what? After all that thinking and overthinking and wondering and hurting, I still don't know. I guess maybe it helps that you don't really know either."

The green clock says only six minutes have passed since I was looking at it, at the sink I never would have allowed a decade ago. Six minutes. I wonder how long it took for him to make the decision that would change us, and then I wonder at the futility of me wondering something like that.

"I can't change what you did. You hurt me so badly. But

you hurt yourself worse maybe." I notice his slumped shoulders, his eyes watching the floor.

"I used to be so afraid of you not loving me. Of you changing your mind again. I thought, if I just kept everything just right, if everything was perfect, then you would stay."

"Danny, I -"

"No, there's no argument. It was too long ago to argue about anymore. I'm saying I was wrong. There was no holding you. What you did, that was on you. It wasn't because of anything I did or didn't say or did or didn't do or whatever."

"Of course it wasn't." He's looking at me again, his eyebrows drawn up, and I smile at remembering watching those lines appear in the corners there.

"Do you know how long it took me to realize that?"

"I can't imagine."

"Years. A lot of years. The therapy helped, I guess, but even then, years and years passed before I figured it out. The reason you cheated. The reason you broke us."

"I'm sorry, you know. I really am."

"You've said you're sorry a million times."

"A million and one, then."

I shake away his apology with the toss of my head. "The reason… There was no real reason. I didn't screw up. I didn't make you do what you did. I wasn't perfect, but there was no reason. Thank god you figured that out today."

He finally moves to rub that space on the back of his neck again, across to wear it meets his shoulder. He should book himself a massage maybe.

"Danny -"

I shake my head again. "There's no point in you saying anything anymore. No point."

I move past the fridge. I once thought that fridge would hold pictures drawn by little hands, report cards, little notes, a grocery list so much bigger than the one it holds now. When I lost the chance of that happening, I thought it would maybe hold photographs of our adventures together, love notes between us two.

But the fridge is bare, save for last year's school picture of Jaimie.

"Come on," I say over my shoulder. "If we're going to make it to dinner, we should probably get ready."

CHAPTER 23

Mark, age 65
2038

I always thought my parents would be the first to go. I'm older, after all. But Mom and Dad are okay. In one of those retirement places, and not doing great of course, but still okay.

Calvin called, looking for Danielle of course.

How can I tell her? I've been staring at this phone for the last… Oh god, I don't even know how long it's been. Twenty minutes? Four hours? She's just in the basement, in her dark room, no doubt humming along to some Broadway soundtrack, so happy or at least content with the world. Any minute she's going to come upstairs and I will have to tell her.

It wasn't like we didn't know this day would come. It's incredible at our age to have parents left, let alone all of them. Well, now, almost all of them.

Why did it have to be her mother? Not that I want someone else to be gone, but this rift between them…

I shake my head. We knew it would happen eventually. But you always think there's time.

The last time we saw them it was last Christmas. Or the one

before? No, definitely last Christmas.

Danielle was wearing this long dark blue dress. Her hair is short now, and curled, and has all this silver weaving through it, but of course she dyed it for the occasion. "Going to their house." It was never "going home". I haven't lived at my parents' for forty-five years or more, but before they moved I still said "going home". Danielle's tones are always measured when she talks about them about that place, each word deliberately chosen.

Maybe I should go interrupt her. Would it be less cruel to tell her right away? Or is it better to give her this one last moment?

The sound of her footsteps climbing the stairs removes the need for the question.

I was right. She was humming. Still is, in fact. Before I met her, I never knew that someone could hum out of tune. She can, and does.

There is a sour taste in my mouth hearing the rise and fall of her voice. I don't want to take away her humming.

"Danielle." I call to her. Her humming stops, and it isn't long before she is standing near me, near where I have frozen, my feet moulded to the hardwood. Her hand is on her hip, her head cocked to the side, her eyebrows raised, waiting and looking so regular and fine and damned normal that I still have no idea how I'm going to tell her.

"What is it?" she asks after standing for a moment.

I hear the blood pound through my ears. I keep watching her face, trying to cement in my mind this moment, this "before" moment of the Danielle who hums when she comes up from the dark room, this woman who is confused and probably a little annoyed that I called her into the room and then ignored her.

I must be taking too long to answer. Her hand drops to her side and she straightens. Her lips part and her eyebrows draw together.

How can I tell her? She always acted like she didn't care.

Never wanted to talk about any of it. About her.

But now there's nothing left to say, is there?

"Danielle." My voice is a whisper. I can barely hear it; I'm sure she can't. I try again. "Danielle."

"What is it? Just tell me. You're scaring me."

Best just to say it, I suppose. "Calvin called when you were downstairs."

Her hand rises in slow motion, pressing against her chest. "Yes?" Now she's whispering, too.

"It's your mother. A heart attack, he said. Last night."

Her eyes flutter shut. Her jaw tightens. She nods once, twice, but doesn't open her eyes.

"She's gone? If he called… she's gone?"

"Yes."

Her eyes open then.

"Danny, Honey, I'm so sorry." I can't remember the last time I called her Honey or baby or sweetheart or any of those platitudes. Decades, probably.

I take a step forward, but she steps back at the same minute, shaking her head. "I'm okay. It's okay."

She looks to the side. I'm not sure what she's looking at exactly, but I doubt it's the wall or her photograph hanging there.

"Did Calvin… did he say anything else? Did she say anything before…"

Oh god.

I once believed that I never lied. And then Allison had happened, and I had lied, so many times. I had spent years - decades even - trying to make up for it. I haven't lied to her since.

But now, more than anything else in the world, I wanted to. I wanted to press her face to my chest. I wanted her to empty herself of years of unshed tears and unspoken anger. I wanted her to ruin my shirt with so many tears. Wasn't that supposed to be my job?

But most of all, I wanted to lie to her. I wanted to tell her that yes, Calvin had said her mother had dying words. Her mother had cried, too, over her daughter. She had apologized in her last breaths and sought to make amends. Hell, even that she had railed and yelled out against her. Or just her name. A whispered, tortured breath carrying her daughter's name.

But she hadn't. At least not that anyone knew about.

She had gone to bed early, saying she was feeling tired. She didn't wake up with her husband came into the room. He called the ambulance, but she was gone before they got to the hospital. There weren't last words, as far as anyone knew.

"At least she didn't suffer," I'd offered Calvin on the phone. "Seems it was quick and peaceful. As much as it can be anyway."

Danielle takes my silence as proof of what she already knew. Her mother didn't ask for her.

"When… the funeral? When is it?"

"Next Tuesday. Calvin said you're supposed to phone him, but it can wait till tomorrow or whenever."

"No I can call now." She lifts her chin a bit, but keeps looking at that wall. "The arrangements, you know… There are a lot of arrangements."

"Calvin said she took care of a lot of that already. She had pretty much everything organized."

"And Dad….?"

"Jaimie is there already. Classes don't start for a couple weeks yet, so she went straight there as soon as they heard. And Calvin and Shantelle are going tomorrow."

"Okay." She nods, but doesn't move.

"What can I do? Do you need anything? Want anything? Can I bring you something? Glass of water? Want to sit down?"

She shakes her head. "You sit down, Mark. You're making me dizzy."

"Sorry." I put my hands in my pockets and wait.

"I'm okay. I'm going to go for a walk."

"Do you want me to come with you? Or do you need to be

alone?"

"It doesn't matter." She takes two steps toward the door. "No, actually, I'd rather be alone I think."

"Okay. If you change your mind. If you need anything, just let me know."

I didn't move until I heard the door close, and then I sunk into the overstuffed armchair.

CHAPTER 24

Danielle, age 57
2038

Do you know when you hear a song and you can't really remember the words or anything, but the tune of just the chorus or something gets stuck in your head and that's all that that plays over and over again for days?

That's what was going on as I was down in my dark room, and somewhere between starting the archival rinse and placing the photos on the drying racks, I started to hum that tune.

I think the words may have had something to do with a rainbow.

My grandmother used to sing when she worked around the house, gospel songs, mostly, and old classic country singers. I remember her singing Johnny Cash while gutting a fish in the back sink at her house, remember watching the head fly off with a *thwak*. She sang about walking the line, getting the words mixed up as she slit open the belly and pulled out guts and bones. I remember her singing "Amazing Grace" while dusting, lifting up picture frames of smiling children at birthday parties and families in matching sweaters at Christmas.

But I don't sing.

I hum, and I'm still humming as I head up the stairs. I'm not even to the top when Mark calls me to the living room. I'm about to ask him his plans for lunch, but the expression on his face stops my words.

I wait, but he is standing there, frozen, staring at me. If this was a stranger on the street it would be disconcerting. As it is, I know this man, and I know he is trying to figure out how to tell me something.

The seconds stretch on as I watch his forehead wrinkle in that space between his eyebrows. He bites his lip, looks at me, looks down, bites again. He shifts his weight, back to his heels, up to the balls of his feet, back, then forward, each movement creaking the floor beneath him.

The silence and waiting is just too much. Whatever it is that he needs to tell me, can't, cannot be worse than the possibilities running through my head. Something has to be very wrong with Mark.

Perhaps he cheated. Again. No, I will not allow myself to think that. I know he's faithful now.

I thought I knew he was faithful before, too. Damn me and my worry. Damn him. Damn waiting for whatever this horrible news is. I have to ask.

"What is it?"

He still doesn't answer. This must be bad, really bad. Perhaps the possibilities aren't worse, after all, than whatever the truth is. *Oh god, at least I hope so.*

He whispers my name, and I know that the truth is worse. He repeats it, maybe in some vague attempt to make sure I am listening.

"What is it? Just tell me. You're scaring me."

"Calvin called when you were downstairs."

I know, then. News so bad that it's making Mark's face pale? News delivered by Calvin? Someone was sick, or hurt. Or dead.

Don't be Jaimie. Don't be Jaimie. Don't be Jaimie. Don't be Jaimie.

Don't be -

"It's your mother. A heart attack, he said. Last night."

Oh god.

I know my eyes are closed, because all I see is black. All I hear is my pulse, pounding so fast and so loud it's all I can focus on. I'm sure Mark can hear it, can see the twitching vein in my temple.

I can't open my eyes. I know Mark is still there, watching, making sure I don't faint or have a breakdown or something.

Then, as quickly as a breath, a word, a gasp, it stops.

I'm hollow.

Mom isn't sick, lying in a hospital bed, recovering from this heart attack. Reality sits in my gut, a rat gnawing away at my conscience, hairless pink tail twitching across the years and memories.

I can't open my eyes. One look at Mark will confirm it. But I have to hear it. That rat can't sit in the dark, chewing holes in me.

"She's gone? If Calvin... If he called... she's gone?"

"Yes."

The black behind my eyelids erupts into swirls and grey and sparks. I have to open them or I'm going to be sick.

The world is slanted. Did it look this way before? How are we standing upright? How is everything not crashing to the ground?

"Danny, Honey, I'm so sorry."

Honey. Why is he calling me Honey? When was the last time he did that? I must look bad.

He comes toward me, and I shake my head and step away, still amazed we're both upright. I don't want to be touched right now. Not even sure I can be talked to. I only want - oh, I don't know what I want. But Mark has that horrid worried look, his arms, usually gesturing at every word, hanging limp and immobile at his sides.

"I'm okay. It's okay." I turn my face away.

There's a photograph on this wall, one of mine. A macro

shot of one of the roses Mark brought me home for our anniversary a few years back, some symbol of some bridge we'd crossed.

I'm proud of that picture. The way the light hits it, and the detail...

Why am I not crying? Shouldn't I be crying? Shouldn't I be reliving fond memories, replaying our last conversation, asking details? Bawling my eyes out? That's my mother, for god's sake. *Was* my mother.

"Did Calvin... did he say anything else? Did she say anything before..."

Mark looks down. I don't need the long space or the shake of his head to know she hadn't asked about me, hadn't said anything.

Of course she hadn't. It wasn't that I expected her to, after all. I just wondered.

I need to get out of here.

I wrap my arms around myself instead, digging my nails into the flesh of my arm.

"When's the funeral?" My voice is even. Why am I not crying?

"Next Tuesday. Calvin said you're supposed to phone him, but it can wait till tomorrow or whenever."

I dig my fingernails in deeper and curl them. The pain cuts through me. I lift my chin. *Bring it on,* I challenge my own nails. I have always chewed them, and think now of the thin edges. *Hurt me,* I tell the jagged pieces. *I dare you.* I'm sending telepathic messages to my fingernails, and am acutely aware of how insane that makes me.

"No I can call now. What about the arrangements? There are always so many arrangements with these things."

"Calvin said she took care of a lot of that already. She had pretty much everything organized."

Of course she did.

"And Dad....?" I say out loud.

"Jaimie is there already. Classes don't start for a couple

weeks yet, so she went straight there as soon as they heard. And Calvin and Shantelle are going tomorrow."

"Okay."

Mark is almost vibrating with unspent energy. "What can I do? Do you need anything? Want anything?" He starts pacing now, but his arms still haven't moved. "Can I bring you something? Glass of water? Want to sit down?" The man clearly needs a job.

I shake my head. "You sit down, Mark. You're making me dizzy."

"Sorry." He sits in a nearby chair, on the edge, clasping and unclasping his hands, looking down at his fingers and palms and wrists. He's wearing the watch I gave him three - no, four - Christmases ago. He looks like a puppy that was just chastised. If he had a tail, he would be sulking in the corner with it between his legs.

I need to get out of here, I think again with more urgency. "I'm okay. I'm going to go for a walk."

"Do you want me to come with you?" I swear, his ears prick up. *Walk, boy? Want to go for a walk? Heel!* "Or do you need to be alone?"

"It doesn't matter." I don't want to hurt his feelings. He's trying to help, after all.

On the other hand, I'm not sure that now is the best time for me to be worried about Mark worrying about me. I shake my head. "Never mind. I'd actually rather be alone I think."

I'm leaving as I hear him offer up some invitation at comfort. The words don't really register, but it doesn't really matter. I hear the tone; I understand what he means.

Now that I'm outside though, I'm not sure what I'm supposed to do.

Down the block, I guess.

I turn west, as good a direction as any.

I didn't get to say goodbye.

I never expected to, if I'm honest. I never expected a big reunion or some heartfelt apology. I'm old enough to know that a leopard can't change its spots. Or is the saying about a tiger not changing its stripes? I don't know. Some big cat and some shape.

She'd think I was stupid for not knowing.

I knew that I couldn't stay around her, back then. I knew that.

I also knew she missed me. When I left. When I stayed away. At least I hope she did. But maybe she couldn't stay around me either.

She always wanted more for me than that store, more than the pictures and Mark and a job that just helped with the bills.

I can't blame a mother for wanting good things for her daughter.

She did say she was proud of me once.

I move past the Murakis' place, and the Rankins' dog starts barking from across the street.

She once asked me about the kids thing. Always the kids thing. Always the offhand comments: "Oh, you should see Jane's granddaughter. So sweet." "Did you hear Charles' wife is pregnant again? Their third! Isn't that wonderful?" "Your aunt Melinda never had kids. She's so alone now. That must be miserable." And my personal favourite: "You aren't getting any younger, you know."

But then, one day, there were no comments. Just a question, blunt and straightforward and bare.

And I answered her, blunt and straightforward and bare.

I had beat around the bush for years, shrugging off the comments, hinting that there was more to the story, wanting her to ask as desperately as she no doubt wanted to know.

"No, Mom. There won't be kids."

"So many young people today are deciding not to, putting career first and all that. But I don't understand, Danielle. It's not like you have some great career. Is it Mark? Does he not want kids? That's awfully selfish of him."

"That's not it, Mom."

"I don't understand."

"Sometimes...sometimes nature just makes our decisions for us."

Remembering those words, now, I stop walking, right there on the sidewalk. Do I look old enough to look senile to anyone peering through their window blinds? It doesn't matter.

I'd always thought I told her the truth that day. But I hadn't. I had gotten close to the truth, even close enough maybe, but I hadn't told her the truth. Not really.

I hadn't told her about the box of baby things I still kept in the recesses of the closet. I hadn't told her about the plans I'd made, how I'd started redoing the guest room and choosing names, imagining a high chair pulled up to our table. I hadn't told her about the endless nights I sat up, pouring through books and making lists and plans.

I hadn't told her about that positive test, about surprising Mark with the "#1 Dad" baseball cap when he came home from work that day. It had been waiting in that "one-day" box, of course, waiting for that little plus sign to appear.

I hadn't told her about that, about the vitamins, about cutting out the alcohol and every bit of bad food, about stopping running, about those first blood tests and doctor's appointments.

And I didn't tell her about the afternoon I started bleeding. I didn't tell her about Mark getting called out of a class to take me to the hospital, that for some reason I hadn't driven myself or even called an ambulance. I'd waiting for him, for my husband. The doctor and Mark and everyone else told me that it wouldn't have mattered if I'd gotten there a little quicker; even an hour or two wouldn't have been enough time. But I shouldn't have waited.

I didn't tell her that.

And I didn't tell her about the way the doctor walked in, shaking his head, looking out the window, then at us, that pathetic expression on his face, an attempt at consoling but falling ridiculously, hopelessly, unforgivably short. I didn't tell her about his hand on Mark's shoulder, but how he looked right at me and told me, told us, that she was gone.

It was too early to know if it was a girl, I supposed. But somehow…

Anyway, it doesn't matter now.

I haven't gone very far, but I turn to return to the house anyway.

I wasn't sure about trying again after that. After the miscarriage, I wasn't sure how much more my heart could take.

Quite a bit, it turns out, because then Mark cheated. She didn't know about that, either.

And then, when we finally did start trying again - well, not trying, but not preventing - then nothing happened. I didn't tell her about those months, those years. And then, eventually, it became too late.

What if that was my chance, my one opportunity to be honest with her? I could have allowed myself to be vulnerable with her. I could have confessed feelings, confided in her. I could have trusted her.

I didn't, but maybe I could have tried at least.

I thought I'd done so much just by that one conversation. I thought I'd given some piece of myself, opened up, been honest.

It was my fault, I knew. My fault she didn't talk to me. My fault she forgot about me. My fault that I couldn't forgive her for things that happened when I was a child, for scathing words and slamming doors and bruises and thrown objects and fear and pain and tears.

It was my fault she didn't say anything about me at the end.

My fault that I didn't say goodbye.

I step back into the house, locking the door behind me and kicking off my shoes. Mark is still there, sitting in the chair in the living room. I feel his eyes on me as I move past him, but he makes no effort to talk to me.

The suitcase is in the top of the closet, as always. There is a thick layer of dust on it, and I sneeze as I pull it down.

When I travel, I generally make a list with everything on it I could need. Quantities and items, in two clean columns. I stop short of using a ruler to draw the line down the center. Items are folded and rolled together, placed in just the right spot along the sides and with other items. But now, I'm opening drawers and doors, pulling out enough clothing for a week, piling them in a heap on the center of the open case.

"I need to go," I say aloud, not turning but knowing Mark is listening and watching.

"Call Calvin first."

"I'll call him. But I need to go. I can help Dad or something. Or Jaimie. I don't know who. Or what. But I need to go." I stop then, in front of my closet.

I hear the chair creak as he pulls himself out of it. I hear his feet pad across the floor down the hall and into our room. He's standing in the doorway.

"What are you doing?" he asks, and I keep staring at my closet.

"I have to... I have to find the right thing... The right.... The right dress..."

"The right dress?"

"For the funeral. It needs to be the right one."

"Honey." He steps toward me like I'm some wild animal and he's afraid of being clawed to death. "It doesn't matter what you wear. You can wear whatever you want, whatever makes you comfortable."

He doesn't understand. I shake my head, hard and quick, to show just how much he doesn't understand.

"No. It has to be right. She... She'd want..."

Another step toward me. I start pulling items out. Anything black. Pulling each one out and over my head. I don't bother to pull it down, don't bother to remove my sweater first. Off the hanger, over my head, back off, discarded to the floor.

Something in here has to work.

"Honey..." That word again: *Honey.*

This dress isn't right either. Not that blouse. Not this one. Too gauzy. Not dressy enough. Too young. Too old.

"Danielle." The nearness of him makes me jump. I don't know when he moved to stand beside me, but there he is, in the direct firing line of material and hangers.

I pause, my hand hovering over a red summer dress.

"It doesn't matter what you wear. Your mom will just be glad you came." I gulp. When did it become so hard to breathe?

"You mean glad I showed up because I never showed up in life?"

"No, that isn't what I meant." He lifts his hand and puts in on my shoulder, just like that damn doctor did to him, all those years ago. I try to shrug it off, but I don't try hard enough to actually pull away from his touch.

"You guys had your differences. But she loved you. You loved her. You both knew that. She wouldn't have cared what you wear to her funeral."

"She would have. She always cared what I wore." I think my chest might be caving in. "She always cared. It wasn't right, wasn't good enough. Just once, just once I want to be good enough. The last time... oh god... the last time I see her, I want... I want to be good enough."

There is an invisible hand picking me up and shaking me, crushing me in its grip. I gasp big breaths, ragged and forced.

And then there's Mark's shirt, and my face is pressed into it, and all I can think is how nice he smells, how I have never, never gotten tired of that smell.

It's easier to breathe now. Now that he's holding me together, I know I'm not going to be shaken apart. My chest is most likely not going to cave in.

"She told me she was proud of me once," I tell him. I don't know if he can hear me, with my voice so muffled and my face squeezed so tight to his shirt. But it doesn't matter.

I heard me. And maybe Mom heard me. Maybe she knew that I remembered.

And then, at last, something broke, and I started to cry.

CHAPTER 25

Mark, age 72
2045

The funeral was nice, I guess. Bigger than when Danielle's mother died. Not as big as when her dad did.

And it was good to see the aunts and uncles and cousins again. The ones who are left, anyway.

And Brett, of course. On wife number three. Or is it four? Don't think I'd ever met this one before, but who the hell knows. Maybe I did. Memory isn't what it used to be.

I'd judge, but the only reason I'm still married to wife number one is because she's some kind of saint.

Saint Danielle is sitting there now, in the passenger side, staring out the window.

Mom was there, of course, looking like a little sparrow beside that big coffin. Danielle was the one who went up with her, not me and Brett like it should have been. Danny just jumped up and walked to the front, her back straight, snaking my mother's arm through hers, holding her hand.

Maybe it was better she was with another woman. Better with her than with her sons, the two boys who drove her crazy, who she would worry about, who she would try to be strong for, just like she has our whole lives.

Better she be with someone else. Someone who might understand.

Or will one day.

One day Danielle will be standing there, like Mom was today, looking down at me in a coffin.

Unless she gets me cremated, I guess, which I would be okay with. I don't really care, so she may as well go with whatever is cheaper, unless it is easier for her to put me in a box than a furnace.

Her dress is pretty. She always looks pretty. Always has.

It's black, of course.

Been wearing a lot more black a lot more often these past few years it seems. Probably only going to wear more, too.

Will she wear that same dress for me one day? What will she think of, looking down into that casket? God I hope she doesn't just think of Allison. I hope she remembers something better. A vacation, maybe, not that we took very many. Or making up after a fight. The darkroom I made her. Getting down on one knee in that coffee shop booth. Our wedding day, walking down the aisle. Or hell, remember sitting at our kitchen table eating take-out. I just don't want her to only think of the bad stuff. I don't want her memories to be focused on tears and disappointment, of packing a suitcase and driving away.

Maybe she'll go first. Maybe I'll be standing over her one day.

Statistics say that is not likely, thank god. Don't think I could handle that.

Don't think I could handle saying goodbye.

Dad was sick a long time. I can't do that. Can't deal with her being sick. Can't deal with me being sick like that, watching her watch me be sick.

Maybe when I get bad, really bad, maybe I'll just drive my car off a cliff. If I can still drive, that is.

I grip the wheel a bit tighter.

I can't imagine not being able to drive anymore, but I know the day is creeping closer that they'll take away my license. Damn near killed Dad when they took his. He made some comment about, if we'd had kids, he would have grandkids to at least drive him around.

How convenient that he didn't mention Brett's kids driving him around.

He felt stranded, isolated, after he lost his license. Caged, even.

I don't want to feel that way. I just hope that creeping day stays away for a long while yet.

This train of thought is a little depressing. Guess I should call the conductor or something. Jump from the moving cars onto some other train.

Lots of time left, maybe. Hope so.

I sneak a glance at Danny again. Her elbow is on the ledge of the window, her hand cupping her chin as she watches the houses move past.

There used to be a park up here. We went walking in it a few times. Even had a picnic there once I think. Now it's all houses. That's the way things go. Other places for other people to make memories, to sit at tables and on couches, to fight and make up, to cry and laugh and open presents and slam doors and read books and drink bottles of wine. And hell, some of them might even have picnics in their backyards.

I wonder if Mom and Dad ever went on picnics. I wonder if he ever really messed up. I mean bad, like I did with Allison.

Even if he did, they still made it. She didn't talk about bad stuff today. She talked about the way he brought her flowers when they were dating - courting, she said - and that her father didn't approve of him at first. She talked about their first house, and the way he looked at her when he held their first child. Me. She talked about rough patches, and good years, and that he was a kind, intelligent man who was a good husband and good father.

God I hope Danny remembers the good things when it gets to be my time.

And there were good things. Are good things, I mean. And more to come.

Maybe tomorrow I'll surprise her. Pack a picnic and drive out somewhere where there's a table, and we can sit outside. I might even bring some wine. It's not too late to make more memories for her to pull from when she's standing at the front of a church or funeral home or wherever, looking down at me.

The corners of my mouth twitch up, so I shake the smile away from my face. There is something horribly inappropriate about grinning when I'm driving away from my father's funeral.

But I bet Dad would have loved it.

CHAPTER 26

Danielle, age 69
2050

Jamaica was Jaimie's idea. A girls' trip, she said, with her daughter and her mom and her beloved Auntie Danny. My invite was maybe a pity one, but I was okay with that if it meant sand and palm trees and the ocean and my favourite niece and her daughter.

So when she called and asked if I was interested in the trip, that old suitcase was dusted off and open on my bed before I hung up the phone.

Mark didn't object, of course. He never does.

I know I'm getting "up there" in years, so I probably don't have that many vacations left in me. Not that I've gone on that many in the first place, I suppose.

But then, after the first appointment, and the second, and the third, and the prognosis, I have even fewer.

Mark doesn't know, not yet, anyway. I'm not really sure how to break that news. Do I sit him down first? Tell him over dinner? Do I lead up to it, or just spit it out?

At any rate, I wasn't ready to tell him, so I kept it to myself before Jamaica. During the whole trip, too, I didn't say a word. I said I wasn't going to start treatments right away anyway, if I decide to try at all. The outlook doesn't look too good, the doctors said. I'm not sure if it is worth the pills and the pain and the vomit and the hair loss and the weakness.

Mark isn't one to tell me what to do, but I have a feeling he will have an opinion about the treatments. Maybe that's just as well; if he offers his recommendations loudly enough, maybe I'll listen.

Maybe I need someone to tell me what to do here.

I know medicine has come a long way. Forty, even thirty years ago, I wouldn't be looking at more than a 12% survival rate. But now my chances are as good as 50%.

I'm just not sure that even those chances are good enough.

So I wanted that getaway, that chance to see a part of the world I never have, the chance to watch birds diving into the water, the chance to feel the sun warm my face, the chance to drink a mai tai by the pool, the chance to watch Jaimie's daughter chase the waves, back and forth as they slid onto the sand.

It was a good trip.

But now, now I know I have to tell Mark. I can't avoid it any longer.

He's sitting there, in that easy chair, reading a book. In the last few years he's become really interested in thriller crime stories. Don't understand what he sees in them. I see no interest in reading about murder and kidnapping and whatever else. But he likes them.

His glasses are considerably thicker than they used to be. They sit perched on the edge of his nose, and he looks so much like an old professor I have to stand in the doorway and just smile at the sight of him. All he needs now is a jacket with elbow patches. Maybe next Christmas.

If I'm still around then.

I don't want to disturb him. Maybe I'll come back later.

He looks up, of course, just as I make up my mind to turn away.

"What is it, Danielle?" He's smiling, seeing me there, staring.

"Sorry?"

"Are you going to make a habit of watching me read?" His tone is light, teasing, but I don't laugh.

"Sorry. My mind went away for a bit."

"No doubt still lying on a beach." He turns back to his book.

If I'm going to say something, I have to do it now, before his mind becomes filled with dark alleys and ransom notes and crime scenes. I have to do it now, or I may lose my nerve.

"Mark?"

"Hmmm?"

"I need you to put the book down for a minute or two."

He looks up. I wish my voice wasn't so shaky. I sound old. I sound sick.

He must see something in my face, because he reaches over the side table and grabs a real bookmark, a leather one that Jaimie gave him years ago. She made it in school, I think.

He places the bookmark, straight up and down, with the tiniest bit showing at the top when he closes it. Which he does, and then shifts the bookmark's visible top even more, so it's even.

I used to be the one who liked things "just so." I don't remember when he became so precise. It seems in stark contrast to the messiness I'm about to hit him with.

He's looking at me now, the book sitting on the side table, his hands resting on his knees.

Once, he walked into a room, a hotel room I'd rented after I packed up the same suitcase that now has sand hidden in the creases and corners. The room I'd rented after I left. He told me we needed to talk. He was honest and ripped out my heart and trampled on it and spat on it.

He ruined us then.

But now I know it was a temporary ruin.

This isn't temporary. I know it isn't my fault. But I know it's not temporary.

"What is it?"

He's waiting. I cross to the room and sit on the edge of the chair diagonal from him. I need to look at him once more first, once more before I tell him. Once more before there is nothing but pity and worry left in those eyes every time he looks at me.

So I do.

I look at that face, the one I've woken up to for decades, the one that has cried and yelled and raged, the one that has lied to me and hidden behind text messages and secret meetings and stacks of homework. The one that has begged and pleaded and asked. The one that has loved and kissed, that's pressed itself into me, that's gasped and moaned, that's told me the worst and best things I ever thought I'd hear. That face has become worn now, softer, more lined there, where he furrowed his brows at students' work, and there, where he laughed at our inside jokes.

I open my mouth, but I can't make the words come out.

There it is already. That worry.

Not yet, please not yet. Look at me with love once more, before you look at me with pity. Please. I'm sending my entreaties across the short distance to him, but I'm not sure if he can hear me.

He leans back, still watching. Still worrying, but more with wonder and confusion than anything.

I have no idea how I'm going to begin. Perhaps if I just start talking, I'll find my way there.

"It's funny, you know. Life. When I was a kid I always thought there would be some moment when I would realize I was an adult, some magical time when I'd feel all grown up, when I'd have all the answers. Now I'm nearing the end of my life, and I still feel like a little kid, some twelve-year-old girl sitting around doing her math homework, maybe. That was always the worst."

"Ah, you aren't nearing the end. You've got lots of years left."

I smile, but otherwise ignore him.

"I was always so afraid of being like my parents. They didn't really love each other I don't think. I always thought that was the worst thing."

"After math homework, you mean?" One corner of his mouth twitches, and I wish I had my camera so I could capture that impish little smile.

"Of course. Nothing was worse than math." I feel my smile fall, and I shift. "I think, now, that maybe I was wrong about my parents. Maybe they did love each other. Maybe they just had weird ways of showing it. I never got why they stayed together. But then we stayed together too, and maybe some didn't think we should have."

"You did leave me, remember?"

"I remember."

"That was the worst moment of my life, you know. Coming home and finding you gone. At first I thought my heart would explode, looking all over the house for you. I knew you weren't there, though. I knew as soon as I saw the open closet door and that suitcase gone."

"You remember that?"

"Of course. My heart was racing. And then it stopped. I think that's when it broke."

I am cognizant of the sadness trying to pull down the corners of my lips. "That was a long time ago."

"Yes it was."

"I guess maybe my folks staying together was the right thing, at least for them. I sometimes wondered if me coming back was the wrong thing. But then maybe me leaving was the wrong thing. Me giving up. I didn't know what to do. Go or stay. Come back or not. There was no right answer. Everything seemed   to   be   the   wrong   thing."

"Allison was the wrong thing."

I nod. He'd hear no argument from me on that account.

"Yes, but like I said, all that was a long time ago."

He's nodding now, watching me carefully.

"I always thought we were broken. Beyond repair, then. I was so hurt. Even more than when we - when I - when the baby…"

I clear my throat. "I didn't think I'd ever forgive you. For Allison. I didn't think I'd forgive my mom for staying with my dad when they seemed so miserable. I didn't think I'd forgive myself for leaving, for giving up. And then I didn't think I'd forgive myself for coming back, for giving in. But I did.

"Maybe I wasn't so weak after all. Maybe it was the right thing to do, coming home. Even though everything seemed like the wrong thing, maybe it was all okay. Maybe it was all the right thing to do. Maybe my mom and dad, maybe they stayed together because that was the right thing to do, too."

"Danny…"

"I just want you to know, I guess. I want you to know that I think you're a good man. You've been a good man for most of my life. Most of our life. And we've had some really good times. It's hard to think of those good times, sometimes, because we don't focus on them. We don't focus on the everyday things. I used to love waiting for you to come home from work. I loved being able to make you dinner and watch you sit there marking and muttering away to yourself. And when it got so busy at the store, when I'd come in so tired, from the Christmas rush or whatever, you'd massage my neck and fix me a bubble bath and bring wine and chocolate." I have to clear my throat again. "There are just a lot of good things. It's easy to not think about them when they're happening, 'cause almost every day was a good day. Nothing extreme, I guess. But just coming home to you every day. Just you coming home to me. That's all I ever wanted. Watching my parents all those years ago, hiding Calvin when they'd start screaming and throwing things, all I ever wanted was to come home to a man who wanted me to be there, and for me to want the man to be there too.

"So I guess I'm saying thank you. Thanks for all the good stuff. There's been a lot of good stuff."

I look at him then, at this man who is so much a part of everything about me, who I've hated and loved, and I see his red-rimmed eyes, cloudy and uncertain. His lips are parted and he's staring at me, and I can see his Adam's apple bobbing up and down in his throat.

"Tell me, Danny. Please."

"I love you, Mark. You know that, right? I've always loved you. I want you to know that."

"Jesus Christ Danielle." His words are angry, but his voice is a whisper. He doesn't really want to know. But he needs to. "It's bad, isn't it?"

"Yeah. It's bad."

"How long?"

I shrug. "They can't say for sure."

"Is it... your dad.... he had.... It was cancer. Is that.... Is that what it is?" The tears have spilled over. I see wet trails down his cheeks, into his whiskers. He used to chase around the house, in our much, much younger years, me giggling and squealing when he caught me as he rubbed his whiskers – darker then – against my much softer, smoother skin.

My head shifts up and down, but he doesn't need to see that to know. "Yeah."

I hear the hissing intake of breath.

"Jesus Christ." And he crumbles. He deflates, a cheerful child's balloon, myself the sharp, rusty needle.

I hear myself begin to repeat all the awful platitudes the doctor told me. "There've been a lot of advances in medicine the last decade or so, you know. Even since Dad. There's a chance -"

"Take it."

"There's a chance, but it's not a great one. There's no guarantee."

"Take the goddamn chance. Whatever it is."

I shake my head. "There are treatments. But no promises. And it will all make me very sick. They said… they said I might even be unrecognizable for a while. I won't be myself."

"For a while? So that's temporary?"

"Well, yes, but there's still no guarantee…."

"Why is this even a conversation? I get there's no guarantee. And if you have to change for a while that won't be good of course, but if it means there is even the tiniest chance whatever the treatments are will work, then for god's sake, take the chance."

"Mark…"

"No." He stands up then, looks down at me, and sits back into the chair. "Damn it, Danielle, no. So it's expensive. I'll pay anything, *anything*, if there is even a chance I can keep you. If I can keep you for a year, a day longer, I'll pay whatever they ask."

"That's sweet, but…"

"No. It's not sweet. I'm not being sweet." He's crying still, crying more. "I'm being honest. I don't want to see you sick, but I'll do anything I can. Everything I can. If there's even the smallest chance."

I know I'll take the treatments. I know they'll work for a while, get our hopes up, maybe buy us a few years. But in the end, I'll die. Sick and exhausted, on a hospital bed, I'll die, and he'll watch me. And I don't want him to.

I tell him that.

I tell him that I don't want his last memories of me to be some fragile weak egg shattered and spilt all over a hospital bed, hooked up to machines with hair falling out.

Egg… egg… I've thought of myself as an egg before.

When was that? I remember a booth in a coffee shop. One coffee, one tea. He was there, then.

He was there for pretty much everything.

I tear myself away from memory lane and back to this moment, sitting in this chair, watching this man fall apart.

If I can give him something to keep him together, I will. I

always have; I always will. If that hope, for just a bit more time, is what does it, then so be it.

I'll start treatments next week.

CHAPTER 27

Mark, age 81
2054

Thank god it's a little better right now. I thought I heard her whimpering earlier, but when I went in to check on her she was sleeping. There were dark blotches on her pillow, the cotton darkened from the tears she's poured onto it.

I pad toward the kitchen, pausing at the living room entrance to watch her sleep.

We moved the bed down here a few months ago. Just until this round of treatments is done. Just until she feels better.

Her chest rises and falls, and I try to remind myself that the trembling is normal. That the hitch in each breath is temporary.

Sometimes, especially when she's been crying, she only pretends to be asleep when I come by to check on her. I would never shatter these fictions, not now.

Let her pretend when she wants. Let her cry in private.

But her face is quiet now, her expression soft, her breaths deep despite the trembling and hitching.

In. Out. In. Out. A pause, longer than I would like. In. Out.

In. Out. In…

I continue to the kitchen, filling the kettle and pressing the "on" button on the pad that pops up. Once you had to heat a kettle on a stove. Once you had to plug it into the wall. Once….

Once my wife laughed and danced around and screamed and dreamt of more than her next treatment.

Oh god, please let her still dream of more than her next treatment.

While the water heats, I take the pile of washcloths from the sink to the washer, tossing them in, listening for a sound, any sound, from her corner of the living room.

Always listening, always watching, always waiting.

Never knowing what I'm waiting for.

I take the towels from the dryer, folding them and stacking them into a neat tower that I'll eventually place on the table near her bed, right beside the smaller of the two empty containers on that side. The smaller one goes on the table, the larger on the floor.

She hasn't been able to keep anything down for a few days. Not even water.

Hearing the kettle whistle its silly, artificial notes, I crush the towels under one arm, negating the precise folding I just finished, and head back to the kitchen to stop the sound before it wakes up Danielle.

The kettle off, I steal another peek at her, sleeping there. When she looks this peaceful, this quiet, I am ripped apart between relief and fear. I want her to have some reprieve from the pain, the frustration, the illness, but if she's too peaceful in her sleep…

I shake my head to clear it of its worries.

She'll wake up.

Sure enough, as I set the towels on her table, she shifts, whimpering two notes into the air.

I hate myself for worrying, for not wishing her whatever peace she can find, however temporary.

Or permanent.

Back to the kitchen.

I pull out a mug, one of those novelty ones from some market giveaway. I pour in the hot water, ignoring how my own hand shakes now with the effort of grasping, lifting, holding.

The tea bag drops into the water with a satisfying plop, splashing a few drops over the lip of the cup and onto the counter.

I take my tea, only a shade darker than regular hot water, and move back into the makeshift bedroom, settling into my favourite chair, pulled right upside her bed. The latest detective story is sitting on the seat, right where I left it.

I set my tea on a counter, and bend over Danielle, straightening the blankets around her shoulders, smoothing them over her back, ignoring the bones pushing through her skin and clothes and sheets and comforters and quilts.

It used to be that she couldn't sleep if she was too warm. But now she's never warm enough.

I brush my lips against her bare forehead, the wisps of hair curling above her temples, the hollow of her cheek.

She's still so beautiful.

I settle back into my chair, the detective novel resting on my lap, my mug in my hand.

I could read now, but I won't. At least not yet.

Right now I just want to watch that rise and fall, that trembling, that hitching. I want to watch it all. I want to watch her eyes shift behind her eyelids, watch her lips part and close. I want to be there as soon as she cries out. No, before she cries out.

I want to etch this moment in my mind. This single moment, with her sleeping peacefully, quietly, for a moment without pain but still here, still with me.

I guess maybe I understand a bit why Danielle's always loved taking all those pictures, capturing all those moments. I sure as hell wish I could capture this one.

CHAPTER 28

Mark, age 83
2056

Danielle died three months ago.

Benjamin down the hall has Alzheimer's. We play cards together sometimes. The man can't remember what year it is, or who the hell he is, but he can remember every card I play.

God I wish I could forget what year it is and who the hell I am.

How sick is it that I'm envious of a man who has no idea who the people in the pictures in his room?

Pictures. I have so many pictures of Danny's. Most of them, the ones she printed, are in a big blue plastic box. But a few I have out. A couple albums, a few loose ones up on the bulletin board in my room. A couple framed ones, even. The close-up of the rose, the one of us in Toronto...

She'd get lost looking at art. She'd forget what year it was and who the hell she was sometimes, I think, standing there looking at art.

Sometimes, sometimes when I look at those pictures, sometimes I'm able to forget. Sometimes I'm able to remember.

I'm getting so old. My jaw is even aching now. Goes nicely with my heartburn. Used to be I could eat anything. Used to be nothing slowed me down. Now I damn near shuffle everywhere. There was a time I never even knew a jaw *could* ache.

To be fair, this pain is a new one. But I'm no stranger to others.

Must have eaten something off at dinner. Stomach's sure upset. Because heartburn isn't enough.

Getting old is pretty awful. Wish I'd avoided it.

Almost glad Danny can't see me like this, can't see me with a sore jaw and not able to eat even the blandest food at supper. She'd be rolling her eyes and smiling away, shaking her head at me for being such a big baby.

Her funeral was small. She wanted it that way. That's the thing with fighting cancer for years; you get a lot of time to decide on dying.

I wanted to say something. I told her I would. I told her I was going to recite our wedding vows.

But I couldn't.

She'd gotten all teary when I told her my plan, told me I didn't need to do that, the thought itself was just so lovely that it was all she needed, but god I wanted to.

I even had them put it in the program. Brett told me I wouldn't be able to, and I got so mad at him.

He was right, of course. I was sitting there, had them all typed up, a paper copy and everything, folded up in the front breast pocket of my jacket. I kept watching the program, kept watching that word, "Reading", looming closer and closer.

But I couldn't make myself stand when they finally got to me. I couldn't walk to the front of that tiny church - a church of all things, can you imagine? - and say goodbye to her. My knees wouldn't even let me rise; how could they have held me up?

I threw the paper on the casket at the cemetery instead.

Couldn't say it aloud. Just couldn't. So it's in there with the dirt resting on top of that polished wooden box.

She'd picked it out herself. Thought at first…

God that hurts. My stomach.

Getting too old for anything now.

What was I just thinking about?

Oh yes, Danielle. Always Danielle.

Thinking about how I thought she'd have wanted to be cremated. But her mom and her dad were buried, and she found a plot kind of near them. She said I could choose to do whatever I wanted, but no way I wasn't going to have my final resting place right beside her. So I figured all that out at the same time.

I should probably sit down. Getting a little dizzy. Must be the heat. Or the doctor says I tend to over-exert myself. Apparently walking to my room from the dining room now is over-exertion. I was planning on going to the rec room after dessert, but maybe I should have a nap first.

A little nap does so much good.

I take one of Danielle's albums with me to bed. I don't bother to pull down the covers and sheets, or to undress. It's just a quick rest. Just a little break.

I missed Allison when we split up. It was the right thing to do, of course. Should never have been with her. But I missed her when we were done.

I missed teaching too, when I left. There was a hole in me teaching filled. I missed the kids and the work and making a difference. Or at least feeling like I did.

I missed my dad so much when he was gone. And Mom, that sweet, strong woman.

Danielle was a lot like her, come to think of it.

Nothing compares to how much I miss her. Every goddamn day.

Every…

I wonder if Benjamin misses people? Misses things he doesn't know he's missing?

Goddamn.
Every day.
She was so talented.
This book.
Beautiful.
Yes, a nap.
It will do me good.
Beauti...
One day.
One day she's going to go see the world.
And take pictures of it.
She told me so once.

ACKNOWLEDGMENTS

When I was little, I wanted to be a writer. I didn't know that by scribbling away with crayons and pencils, I already was one. My dear thanks to my parents, siblings, and other family members and teachers, who starred in those first attempts, supplied those materials, dealt with my bookworm tendencies and shaped who I am. You've meant so much.

Thank you to Sharon Umbaug from The Writer's Reader, who provided editorial service which was invaluable and helped elevate this manuscript from beyond the equivalent of a shrug. Further appreciation goes to my local writing group, who've given so much advice and guidance. Thank you, too, to my beta readers, who provided amazing feedback, and caught some errors I'm embarrassed to have missed! I am blessed to know some truly generous people, who gave their time to read my little manuscript and answer my questions. Thank you.

A lot of jokes are made about in-laws, but I'm so fortunate to have married into such a great family. My mother-in-law, Karen MacDonald, is the talented artist who created the beautiful artwork used for my front cover. Thank you! It's perfect.

Thank you to my friends and coworkers, who had to hear updates and whining, who were among the first who heard of this endeavor, who supported and never acted annoyed when I went on and on and on. Thank you to my students, past and present, who continuously remind me why I love that crazy effect of words on a page.

Finally, and most importantly, more thanks than I can ever express to my best friend, my favorite human, who I get to share every day with. The second I thought I wanted to actually try to write this book, my husband told me, "Yes. You should." So I did. Thank you for listening to every single development and setback in this adventure, and in every adventure. Thank you for supporting me, and for reading a book you'd never in a million years pick up if it wasn't my name on the cover. I have no words.

To all of those I've neglected to mention by name, my apologies and appreciation. You know who you are, I hope. You've inspired and supported and just been plain awesome. Thank you.

ABOUT THE AUTHOR

Krysta MacDonald writes about realistic characters confronting the moments and details that make up lives and identities.

She lives in a small Canadian town in the Rocky Mountains with her husband and veritable zoo of pets. She has a B.A. in English and a B.Ed. in English Language Arts Education, and spends most of her time teaching, prepping, marking, and extolling the virtues of Shakespeare. When she isn't doing that, she's writing, and when she isn't doing that, she's reading.

You can connect with Krysta via her website or social media.

The Girl with the Empty Suitcase is her debut novel.

Website: krystamacdonald.wixsite.com/website
Amazon: amazon.com/author/krystamacdonald
Goodreads: goodreads.com/KrystaMacDonald
Facebook: facebook.com/krystamac.writer
Twitter: twitter.com/KrystaMacWrites

CPSIA information can be obtained
at www.ICGtesting.com
Printed in the USA
LVHW111100090719
623549LV00001B/125/P